A CARTOON HISTORY OF TEXAS

by Patrick M. Reynolds

A Republic of Texas Press Book

TAYLOR TRADE PUBLISHING

Lanham • New York • Dallas • Boulder • Toronto • Plymouth, UK

A REPUBLIC OF TEXAS PRESS BOOK

Published by Taylor Trade Publishing
An imprint of The Rowman & Littlefield Publishing Group, Inc.
4501 Forbes Boulevard, Suite 200
Lanham, Maryland 20706

Estover Road
Plymouth PL6 7PY
United Kingdom

Distributed by National Book Network

Library of Congress Cataloging-in-Publication Data

Reynolds, Patrick M.
  A cartoon history of Texas / Patrick M. Reynolds.
    p. cm.
  Includes bibliographical references (p. 321) and index.
  ISBN-13: 978-1-55622-780-6
  ISBN-10: 1-55622-780-9
  1.   Texas—History—Comic books, strips, etc. I. Title.
F387 .R48   2000
976.4'0022'2—dc21   CIP 00-059200

Contents

Part One—Early Texas

Dinosaurs 3
Triassic Texas, 3; Phytosaur, 4; Metoposaur, 5; The
Texas Tech Dinosaur, 6

Indians 7
The Nabedache Indians, 7; Caddo Lake, 8; The
Tawakoni Indians, 9

The Spaniards 10
The Friars' Silver Digs, 10; First Thanksgiving Day,
11; The Hardship Expedition, 12; A Magnificent
Feast, 13; The Old Spanish Roads, 14; The Texarkana
Trading Post, 15; The Irish Conquistador, 16;
O'Connor's Presidios, 17

Part Two—The Era of the Filibusters

Filibuster. 20-21

Philip Nolan 22
The Irish Mustanger, 22; Dreams of an Empire, 23;
The First American Filibuster, 24; The Dice of
Death, 25; The Survivor, 26; Col. Peter Ellis Bean, 27;
Map and Summary, 28, 29

The Louisiana Purchase 30

The Neutral Ground 31

The Magee-Gutierrez Expedition. 32
The Enforcer, 32; The Republican Army of the
North, 33; The Magee-Gutierrez Expedition, 34; The
Siege of La Bahia, 35; The Mysterious Death of
Magee, 36; Ambush at El Rosillo, 37; Prelude to an
Atrocity, 38; The Massacre at La Tablita, 39;

Twilight of a Revolution, 40; A Trap, 41; Map and Summary, 42

Pirates. 44

Jean Lafitte, 44; Louis-Michel Aury, 45; License to Steal, 46; Francisco Xavier Mina, 47; The Battle of Venadito, 48; Getting Rid of Aury, 49; Campeachy, 50; Pirate of the Gulf, 51; The Ultimatum, 52; The Fall of Lafitte, 53

General Andrew Jackson 54

The Adams-Onis Treaty 55

The James Long Filibuster Expedition 56

The Filibuster Army, 56; Another Republic of Texas, 57; The Old Stone Fort, 58; Filibuster Trading Posts, 59; The Filibuster and the Pirate, 60; Knocking Off the Filibusters, 61; Collapse of the Republic, 62; Escape Across the Sabine, 63; International Incident, 64; Fort Las Casas, 65; Jane Wilkinson, 66; Jane Long, 67; Reunited...briefly, 68; Coming Apart, 69; Determination, 70; Long's Second Attempt, 71; Preparations, 72; The President Without a Country, 73; The Commander-in-Chief, 74; A Slight Case of Mutiny, 75; The Last Filibuster, 76; The Taking of La Bahia, 77; The Short Siege, 78; Emperor Augustin I, 79; The "Execution," 80; She Who Waits, 81; Map and Summary, 82, 83

Mrs. Jane Long 84

Standoff at Bolivar Point, 84; The Mother of Texas, 85; "We Regret to Inform You," 86; Baby Mary Long, 87; Jane's Boarding Houses, 88; Jane's Plantation, 89; Kiamata, 90

Part Three—The Era of the Empresarios

Moses Austin 94

The Austin Family, 95; Missouri-Bound, 96; The Fancy Duds Parade, 97; Austin's Company Town, 98; Young Stephen Austin, 99; Fatherly Advice, 100; College, Business, & Politics, 101; Lead and Marriage,

102; Financial Ruin, 103; The Real Power in Spanish
Texas, 104; Chance Encounter, 105; Baron Felipe
Enrique Neri de Bastrop, 106; Bastrop's Sales Pitch,
107; The Provincial Council, 108; Ruined Health, 109;
Arrangements, 110; Dying Request, 111

Stephen Austin 112
The Spanish Escort, 112; Stephen Takes Over, 113;
Austin's Exploration, 114; Juan Erasmo Seguin, 115;
Jonesborough, 116; Red River Port, 117; Land First
Rate, 118; The Plan, 119; Lively, 120; "Muldoon
Catholics," 121; To Qualify as a Texan, 122; The First
Colonist, 123; Andrew Robinson, 124; Waiting for the
Lively, 125; The Lost Colonists, 126; What Happened
to the Lively, 127; Good News & Bad News, 128;
Comanche Hold-Up, 129; Comanche No Fight
Americans, 130; The Tattered Travelers, 131; Austin
Arrived in Mexico, 132; The Waiting Game, 133; Time
Well Spent, 134; Triumph! 135; Picking Up the Pieces,
136; The Old 300, 137; Jared Ellison Groce, 138; The
First Texan of Wealth, 139; The First Cotton Gin in
Texas, 140; San Felipe de Austin, 141; Austin's
Capital, 142; Barter Economy, 143; Empresario, 144;
The First Rangers, 145; Stephen Austin's
Government, 146; Public Education, 147; The Bachelor
Father of Texas, 148

The Rush to Colonize 149

The Empresario Grants 150

The Irish Empresarios 151

Green DeWitt 152
DeWitt's Colony, 153; Gonzales, 154

Martin De Leon 155
The Mexican Empresario, 156; DeLeon's Colony, 157;
Victoria, 158; Overlapping Colonies, 159; The Tobacco
Incident, 160; DeWitt's Arrest, 161; The Downfall of
DeWitt's Colony, 162

German Immigrants 163

Ernst's Place, 164; The First Permanent German
Settlement in Texas, 165

Robertson's Colony 167
Leftwich's Grant, 167; Nashville Company, 168; The
Austin & Williams Contract, 169; Robertson's Colony,
170

The Fredonia Rebellion. 172
One of the Wildest Incidents, 172; Haden Edwards'
Ultimatum, 173; Who's in Charge?, 174; The Republic
of Fredonia, 175; The Fredonian Rebellion, 176; The
Fall of Fredonia, 177

Part Four—People and Places

Characters 181
Smugglers, 181; Lincoln's Partner, 182; Georgetown,
183; Our First Senators, 184; The Swiss Merchant,
185; Fancy Squirts, 186; The First Cowboy Strike,
187; From Gunslinger to Lawyer, 188; The Baker, 189

Entertainers 190
The Crack-Shot Cartoonist, 190; Orchid of the Silver
Screen, 191; Country Music Meets Jazz, 192

Sports 193
Play Ball!, 193; Honest John McCloskey, 194; Louis
"Top" Santop, 195; Women Playing Hardball, 196

Forts and Military 197
The First Frontier Fort, 197; Fort Inge, 198; Fort
Ewell, 199; A Lousy Location, 200; Fort Cibolo, 201;
Milton Faver, 202; The First Texan at West Point,
203; General Randal, 204; Randall County, 205; the
Texas 9th Infantry Regiment, 206

African-Texans 207
Runaway Slaves, 207; Wild Cat and the Escape, 208;
The Quilt Code, 209; Going to Pot, 210; Matthew
Gaines, 211; Amid the Impeachment, 212

Colleges 213

Sul Ross State, 213; Lawrence Sullivan Ross, 214; The Era of Good Feeling, 215; the First Land-Grant College in Texas, 216; An Innovative College, 217; The First School of Nursing, 218; Liz the Librarian, 219

Places. 220

The Aransas Pass Lighthouse, 220; The Rabbit, 221; The Floating Capital, 222; The Elissa, 223; William Henry Hamblen, 224; The Palo Duro Highway, 225; The Bluebonnet, 226, Dangerous Snakes, 227; Beneath the Lone Star, 228; Powell's Cave, 229; Yuletide Places, 230; Good Ol' St. Nicholas, 231; Smeltertown, 232; Name Dropping, 233; Hondo, 234; A Popular Sign, 235

Counties 236

From Seat to Seat, 236; Bosque County, 237; Comal County, 238; Delta County, 239; Dimmit County, 240; Frio County, 241; Hale County, 242; Hartley County, 243; LaSalle County, 244; Limestone County, 245; Milam County, 246; Sterling County, 247; Willacy County, 248

Part Five—The Big "D"

Map of Dallas Metropolitan area, 250; This Was Dallas, 252; Early Visitors, 253

The Founding of Dallas 254

John Neely Bryan, 254; Bryan's Bluff, 255; Bird's Fort, 256; The Founders of Dallas, 257; It Was Almost Called Warwick, 258; The Gilbert Family, 259; Bryan's Contest, 260; Polk, Dallas, and Texas, 261; The Old Preston Trail, 262

La Reunion 263

Socialist Colony, 263, Au Texas, 264; Cantagrel, 265; La Reunion, 266; La Reunion Failed, 267; The Last of La Reunion, 268

The Texas State Fair 269

Sports in Dallas 271

Contents

Strikes, Spares, and Sins, 271; The Bowling
Champion, 272; When the NFL Came to Dallas, 273;
The Dallas Texans, 274; Try, Try Again, 275

Part Six—Texas in the 20th Century

Lumbering 279

Aviation. 282
The Czech Aeronaut, 282; A Blacksmith's Biplane,
283; Barron Field, 284; The Flying Stinsons, 285;
Famous Aviator, 286; Stinson School of Flying, 287

Stay Tuned 288

Paving the Way. 289

Ma and Pa Ferguson 290
James Ferguson, 290; Farmer Jim, 291; "Pa"
Ferguson's Good Works, 292; A Term for the Worse,
293; Farmer Jim vs. the Intellectuals, 294;
Indictment, 295; Impeachment, 296; The Verdict,
297; After His Impeachment, 298; The Ferguson
Ranch, 299; The Slow Road to Recovery, 300; Plan for
a Comeback, 301; The Get Even Candidate, 302; The
First Woman Elected Governor, 303; Pardon Me,
Governor, 304; More Scandals, 305; Honeymoon
Campaign, 306; Governor Dan Moody, 307; Tycoon
Governor, 308

The Great Depression 309
The Fat Boy, 309; Can You Spell H-A-T?, 310; Lighting
Up the Lone Star, 311; Electrified, 312; Farewell to
the Fergusons, 313; The CCC, 314; The Soil Soldiers,
315; The CCC and State Parks, 316; They Were Not
Just Work Camps, 317; Summer Soldiers, 318

World War II 319
The Rattlesnake Bomber Base, 319; The Texans Who
Ran the War, 320

Bibliography 321

Index. 323

Introduction

Except for the maps, each page in this book originated as a weekly feature called "Texas Lore," which appeared every Sunday in the Texas and Southwest section of the *Dallas Morning News* between 1995 and 2000. Running since 1982, these cartoons have already been published in twelve volumes. For collectors, this book represents volumes thirteen through eighteen. Therefore, each of the six sections in this book represents a volume.

Sections two and three give a basic overview of Texas history for the first third of the nineteenth century up to the eve of the Texas Revolution. The action during that era takes place in east and south-central Texas. The other sections cover the rest of the state. Since Texas is so huge, there are maps at the beginning of each section to show the location of each place mentioned in that particular section.

Part One

Early Texas

This map shows the location of the places mentioned in this section.

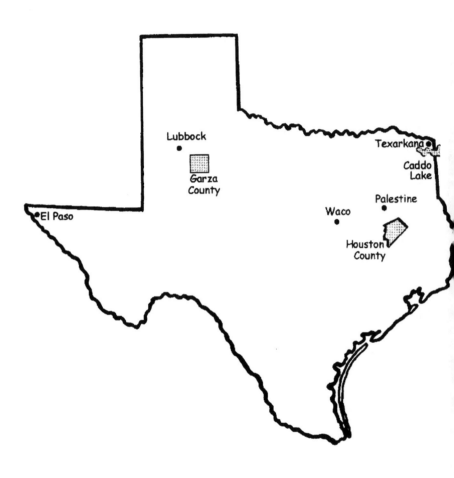

TRIASSIC TEXAS

IT IS BELIEVED THAT 200 MILLION YEARS AGO—THE LATE TRIASSIC PERIOD—THE EARTH'S LAND MASSES CAME TOGETHER AND FORMED A GREAT SUPERCONTINENT CALLED **PANGEA.**

A THIRD OF WHAT IS NOW TEXAS WAS UNDER WATER.

THE EARLIEST KNOWN DINOSAURS IN TEXAS GO BACK TO 220 MILLION YEARS AGO.

FOSSILS OF THESE CREATURES WERE FOUND IN THREE AREAS: THE PANHANDLE, CENTRAL TEXAS, AND THE BIG BEND.

ABOUT 225 TO 220 MILLION YEARS AGO THE PANHANDLE OF
TEXAS WAS PART OF AN INLAND TROPICAL BASIN
SURROUNDED BY MOUNTAINS.

THIS STEAMY MARSHLAND WAS HOME TO AN AQUATIC REPTILE
THAT GREW TO A LENGTH OF SIXTEEN FEET AND WAS KNOWN A
THE

PHYTOSAUR,

WHICH MEANS **PLANT LIZARD.**

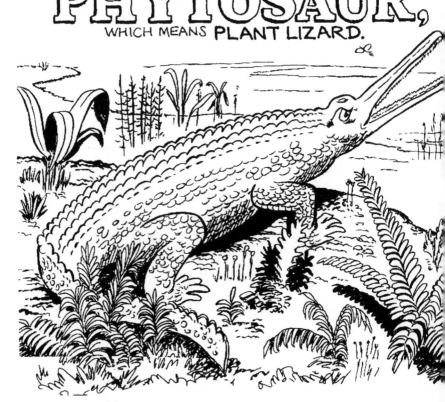

PHYTOSAURS BECAME EXTINCT AT THE END
OF THE TRIASSIC PERIOD, ABOUT 208 MILLION YEARS AGO.

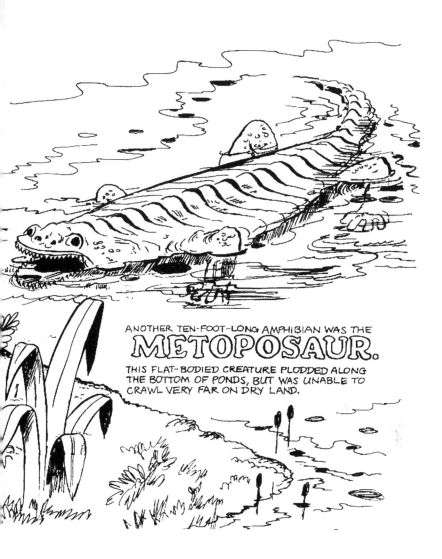

ANOTHER TEN-FOOT-LONG AMPHIBIAN WAS THE

METOPOSAUR.

THIS FLAT-BODIED CREATURE PLODDED ALONG
THE BOTTOM OF PONDS, BUT WAS UNABLE TO
CRAWL VERY FAR ON DRY LAND.

The Texas Tech Dinosaur

FOSSILS REVEAL THAT TEXAS WAS THE HOME OF A VARIETY OF DINOSAURS. THE EARLIEST KNOWN OF THE LONE STAR LIZARDS LIVED IN WEST TEXAS DURING THE LATE TRIASSIC PERIOD, 225 TO 220 MILLION YEARS AGO.

THIS SMALL PLANT EATER, THE SIZE OF A LARGE DOG, WAS FOUND AT THE POST QUARRY IN GARZA COUNTY.

UH-OH...

THE ARCHAEOLOGIST WHO DISCOVERED IT, DR. SANKAR CHATTERJEE, WAS A PROFESSOR AT TEXAS TECH UNIVERSITY IN LUBBOCK, SO HE NAMED THE CREATURE *TECHNOSAURUS SMALLI.*

THE NATURAL ENEMY OF *TECHNOSAURUS* WAS THE 10 FT. LONG MEAT-EATER, *COELOPHYSIS.*

THE NABEDACHE INDIANS,

A HASINAI-CADDOAN GROUP, LIVED NEAR THE HEADWATERS OF THE NECHES RIVER IN PRESENT-DAY HOUSTON COUNTY.

THE FIRST REPORT OF THIS TRIBE WAS MADE IN 1686 BY HENRI JOUTEL, THE SECRETARY OF SIEUR de LA SALLE.

IN MAY 1690 FRAY MASSANET AND DOMINGO RAMON FOUNDED THE SAN FRANCISCO de los TEJAS MISSION IN THE MAIN VILLAGE OF THE NABEDACHES.

ACCORDING TO LEGEND, A CADDO CHIEF FAILED TO OBEY THE GREAT SPIRIT WHO GOT ANGRY AND STARTED AN **EARTHQUAKE**, FORMING **CADDO LAKE.**

ACTUALLY THIS **LARGE** LAKE IN THE SOUTHWEST WAS ONCE A LOG JAM ON THE RED RIVER.

AROUND 1900 THE CORPS OF ENGINEERS DESTROYED THE JAM AND BUILT A DAM NEAR MOORINGSPORT, LOUISIANA, WHICH FORMED THE PRESENT CADDO LAKE IN TEXAS.

THE TAWAKONI INDIANS,

MEMBERS OF THE WICHITA NATION, ENTERED TEXAS FROM OKLAHOMA IN 1700.

THEIR TERRITORY RANGED FROM PRESENT-DAY PALESTINE TO WACO.

ATHANASE MEZIERES, THE SON-IN-LAW OF LOUIS ST. DENIS, WAS THE SPANISH AGENT FOR INDIANS IN NORTH TEXAS. IN 1770 HE NEGOTIATED A TREATY WITH THE TAWAKONIS.

BY THE MID 1800s THE TAWAKONIS WERE IMPOVERISHED. THEY MOVED TO THE WICHITA RESERVATION IN 1859.

The Friars' Silver Digs

FRANCISCAN FRIARS ARE CREDITED WITH THE DISCOVERY OF **SILVER** IN TEXAS AROUND 1680. THEY SECRETLY MINED THE ORE NEAR **EL PASO** FOR SEVERAL YEARS.

FEARING THE JESUITS WOULD TAKE OVER THEIR MINES, THE FRANCISCANS CONCEALED THEIR ENTRANCES AND ABANDONED THEM.

IN JULY 1793 ONE MINE NEAR EL PASO WAS REOPENED AND WORKED UNTIL THE MEXICAN REVOLUTION IN 1821.

MORE THAN TWO DECADES BEFORE THE ENGLISH PILGRIMS SET FOOT ON THE EAST COAST, THE SPANISH CELEBRATED AMERICA'S

first Thanksgiving Day.

IN TEXAS. HERE IS HOW IT CAME ABOUT. IN 1595 THE VICEROY OF NEW SPAIN DECIDES TO ESTABLISH SETTLEMENTS IN WHAT IS NOW NEW MEXICO.

ON APRIL 30, 1598 A CARAVAN DEPARTS SANTA BARBARA, MEXICO.

LEADING THE 400 SPANIARDS IS THE GREAT-GRANDSON-IN-LAW OF MONTEZUMA, **JUAN de OÑATE.** SOMEWHERE IN THE CHIHUAHUA DESERT THE EXPEDITION VEERS OFF COURSE.

The Hardship Expedition

JUAN de ONATE AND 400 SPANIARDS ARE ON THEIR WAY TO COL-
ONIZE NEW MEXICO IN 1598 WHEN THEY WANDER OFF COURSE.
STRUGGLING ACROSS THE CHIHUAHUA DESERT, THEY SOON RUN
OUT OF FOOD AND WATER.

THEY SURVIVE
ON BERRIES,
ROOTS, AND
WATER FROM
CACTI AND OTHER
PLANTS.

AFTER FOUR DAYS WITHOUT FOOD AND WATER THE SPANIARDS
MEET A GROUP OF MANSO INDIANS JUST SOUTH OF PRESENT-
DAY **EL PASO.** THE INDIANS QUICKLY HELP THE STRANGERS AND
GIVE THEM FISH AS A SIGN OF FRIENDSHIP.

IN THE SPRING OF 1598 JUAN de ONATE AND HIS STARVING EXPEDITION REACH THE RIO GRANDE NEAR EL PASO. THE MANSO INDIANS (ALSO KNOWN AS THE JUMANOS) HELP THE SPANIARDS RECOVER FROM DEHYDRATION AND STARVATION. THEN THE INDIANS AND CONQUISTADORS KILL SOME GAME, CATCH SOME FISH, AND GIVE THANKS WITH

A MAGNIFICENT FEAST.

THIS IS AMERICA'S **FIRST THANKSGIVING** OBSERVANCE.

THE PRIESTS CELEBRATE MASS AND ONATE CLAIMS THE LAND—WESTERN U.S.—FOR SPAIN.

SEVERAL OF THE SOLDIERS PUT ON A PLAY WHICH IS THE FIRST THEATRICAL PERFORMANCE IN AMERICA.

The Old Spanish Roads

THIS MAP ROUGHLY SHOWS THE ROUTES USED BY SPANISH EXPEDITIONS INTO TEXAS DURING THE LATE 1600s AND EARLY 1700s.

HISTORIANS GLEANED THESE ROADS FROM DIARIES WHICH THE SPANISH CROWN ORDERED KEPT BY EACH EXPEDITION.

THE DIARIST USED A COMPASS TO NOTE THE DIRECTION OF MARCH AND THE EXPEDITION LEADER TOLD HIM THE DISTANCE TRAVELED EACH DAY.

THESE DIARIES BECAME OFFICIAL SPANISH DOCUMENTS, SIGNED UNDER OATH BY THE DIARISTS.

The Texarkana Trading Post

THE FRENCH TRIED TO MAKE INROADS IN TEXAS BY SENDING BERNARD de la HARPE TO OPEN A TRADING POST ALONG THE RED RIVER ABOVE PRESENT-DAY TEXARKANA IN 1719.

THEIR CLIENTS WERE THE CADDOES, TAWAKONIS, TONKAWAS, AND WICHITAS. BUSINESS WAS SO GOOD THAT THE TRADING CENTER SOON GREW INTO FORT ST. LOUIS.

ARCHAEOLOGISTS UNEARTHED OVER 250,000 FRENCH AND CADDO ARTIFACTS AROUND THIS SITE.

O'CONNOR'S PRESIDIOS

MAJOR HUGO O'CONNOR, NEW SPAIN'S INSPECTOR GENERAL, FOUND DEPLORABLE CONDITIONS IN THE PRESIDIOS IN TEXAS IN 1767. SOLDIERS WERE POORLY ARMED AND EQUIPPED, MORALE WAS LOW, AND THERE WERE NOT ENOUGH TROOPS TO MAN ALL THE FORTS.

O'CONNOR TOOK ACTION. HE CLOSED SOME OF THE LESS DEFENSIBLE PRESIDIOS. THEN HE SET UP A LINE OF PRESIDIOS EXTENDING ALMOST 1,000 MILES FROM LA BAHIA IN TEXAS TO SANTA GERTRUDIS de ALTAR NEAR THE GULF OF CALIFORNIA. THEY WERE GARRISONED BY AN AVERAGE OF 100 MEN TO A PRESIDIO.

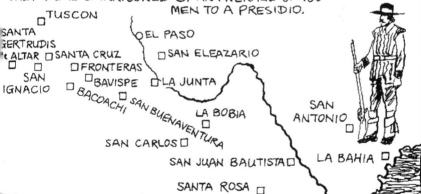

TUSCON

SANTA GERTRUDIS de ALTAR SANTA CRUZ

SAN IGNACIO BACOACHI BAVISPE SAN BUENAVENTURA

FRONTERAS

EL PASO

SAN ELEAZARIO

LA JUNTA

LA BOBIA

SAN CARLOS

SAN JUAN BAUTISTA

SANTA ROSA

SAN ANTONIO

LA BAHIA

Part Two

The Era of the Filibusters

1800 to 1822

Decades before the Texas Revolution of 1836, these men organized and equipped their own armies and tried to take control of Texas.

They were called FILIBUSTERS.

PHILIP NOLAN

AUGUSTUS MAGEE

SAMUEL KEMPER

BERNARDO GUTIERREZ

DR. JAMES LONG

THE TERM

Filibuster

CAME FROM THE ENGLISH WORD *FREEBOOTER*–OR SEA PIRATE. THE FRENCH CHANGED IT TO *FILIBUSTIER* (LAND PIRATE) MEANING PEOPLE WHO STOLE HUGE PARCELS OF LAND OR TREASURE FROM A COUNTRY.

THE SPANISH USED THE WORD *FILIBUSTERO* TO DESCRIBE AMERICAN **ADVENTURERS** WHO TRIED TO **STEAL TEXAS** FROM THE SPANISH CROWN.

SOME, LIKE LT. AUGUSTUS MAGEE, WANTED TO SET UP A TEXAS EMPIRE; OTHERS LIKE SAM KEMPER WANTED TO ANNEX TEXAS TO THE U.S.; WHILE STILL OTHERS LIKE DR. & MRS. JAMES LONG WANTED TO MAKE IT A REPUBLIC.

THE FILIBUSTER ERA LASTED FROM 1800 TO 1821. ALL OF THEIR ESCAPADES FAILED AND MOST OF THE FILIBUSTERS WERE KILLED.

The Irish Mustanger

BORN 1771 IN BELFAST, IRELAND **PHILIP NOLAN** IMMIGRATED TO KENTUCKY IN 1778. AROUND 1791 HE CAME TO THE SPANISH PROVINCE OF TEXAS TO ENGAGE IN THE HIGHLY DANGEROUS AND ILLEGAL TRADE OF *MUSTANGING*—CAPTURING WILD HORSES AND SELLING THEM THROUGHOUT THE SOUTHERN UNITED STATES.

HE SCOUTED TEXAS THOROUGHLY AND MADE THE FIRST MAP OF IT IN ENGLISH. IN HIS TRAVELS NOLAN CONVINCED HIMSELF THAT THE SPANISH OVERLORDS WERE WEAK AND THEIR PROVINCE COULD BE TAKEN FROM THEM.

IN 1797 HE PRESENTED HIS MAP TO BARON de CARONDELET, THE FRENCH GOVERNOR OF LOUISIANA AND RECEIVED A CONTRACT TO "GATHER" HORSES IN TEXAS AND SELL THEM TO THE LOUISIANA REGIMENT.

Dreams of an Empire

IN THE FALL OF 1799 PHILIP NOLAN WENT TO THE UNITED STATES AND WAS GRANTED AN INTERVIEW WITH VICE-PRESIDENT JEFFERSON. SUPPOSEDLY NOLAN OFFERED TO STEAL TEXAS FROM THE SPANISH AND TURN IT OVER TO THE U.S.

A MONTH LATER NOLAN MARRIED FRANCES LINTOT IN NATCHEZ, MISSISSIPPI, BUT LEFT HER IN THE SPRING OF 1800 TO RETURN TO THE FRONTIER.

ACCORDING TO SOME ACCOUNTS-- IN THE SUMMER OF 1800 GENERAL JAMES WILKINSON OF THE U.S. ARMY ENCOURAGED NOLAN TO RECRUIT SOME MEN TO "DETACH TEXAS FROM NEW SPAIN."

MEANWHILE, THE TEXAS GOVERNOR, JUAN de ELGUEZABAL, SUSPECTED THAT NOLAN WAS PLANNING TO START A REVOLUTION AND MAKE HIMSELF **KING OF TEXAS.** HE ISSUED ORDERS TO ARREST NOLAN IF HE ENTERED TEXAS.

The First American Filibuster

IN OCTOBER 1800, PHILIP NOLAN REENTERED TEXAS NEAR NACOGDOCHES WITH ABOUT TWENTY ARMED MEN AND SOME SLAVES, OSTENSIBLY "TO ROUND UP SOME MUSTANGS."

THE SPANISH GOVERNOR SUSPECTED NOLAN OF BEING A FILIBUSTER-**LAND PIRATE**-AND ORDERED HIS ARREST. A HUNDRED CAVALRYMEN TRACKED HIM TO A SPOT NORTH OF **WACO**. NOLAN REFUSED TO SURRENDER.

LT. MUSQUIZ'S MEN OPENED FIRE ON THE AMERICANS' CRUDE LOG FORT AND ONE OF THE FIRST SHELLS KILLED NOLAN. THE REST OF HIS MEN WERE CAPTURED AND SENT TO PRISON IN MEXICO.

NOLAN COUNTY IN CENTRAL WEST TEXAS WAS NAMED AFTER HIM

THE DICE OF DEATH

PHILIP NOLAN'S ATTEMPT TO STEAL TEXAS FROM SPAIN ENDED IN A BATTLE NEAR WACO IN 1800. NOLAN WAS KILLED AND TWENTY OF HIS MEN WERE IMPRISONED, FIRST IN SAN ANTONIO, THEN CHIHUAHUA, MEXICO.

AFTER SEVEN YEARS, THE KING OF SPAIN DECREED THAT EVERY FIFTH MAN BE HANGED AS A PIRATE, AND THE REST SENT TO TEN YEARS OF HARD LABOR. HOWEVER, ALL BUT NINE HAD DIED IN PRISON, SO THE WARDEN DECIDED THEY THROW DICE. EPHRAIM BLACKBURN THREW THE LOWEST, AND FATAL, NUMBER.

BLACKBURN WAS HANGED. THE REST WERE TRANSFERRED TO A PRISON IN ACAPULCO AND NEVER HEARD FROM AGAIN... EXCEPT ONE MAN.

THE SURVIVOR

PETER ELLIS BEAN WAS 17 YEARS OLD WHEN HE JOINED NOLAN'S FILIBUSTER EXPEDITION INTO TEXAS. WHEN NOLAN WAS KILLED, BEAN AND 19 OTHERS WERE CAPTURED. BY 1807 HE WAS ONE OF EIGHT THAT WERE STILL ALIVE IN A JAIL IN ACAPULCO, MEXICO.

WHEN THE REVOLUTION AGAINST THE SPANISH BROKE OUT IN 1810, BEAN WAS PRESSED INTO THE ROYALIST ARMY.

AT THE FIRST OPPORTUNITY, HE DESERTED TO THE REBELS AND ROSE TO THE RANK OF COLONEL IN THE REPUBLIC OF MEXICO ARMY.

THE REBELS NEEDED ARMS AND AMMUNITION. IN 1814 GENERAL JOSE MORELOS SENT COL. BEAN TO THE UNITED STATES TO SECURE AID AND TO RAISE AN ARMY TO INVADE TEXAS.

COL. PETER ELLIS BEAN

RETURNED TO THE U.S. IN 1814 AND COLLECTED $10,000 FOR THE MEXICAN REVOLUTIONARY ARMY, BUT COULD NOT RAISE AN ARMY TO INVADE TEXAS.

HE TRAVELED TO NEW ORLEANS IN TIME TO FIGHT THE BRITISH IN ANDREW JACKSON'S ARMY.

BEAN RETURNED TO MEXICO IN 1815 AND, FOR HIS SERVICES TO THE VICTORIOUS MEXICAN REBELS, WAS GIVEN A LAND GRANT IN MOUND PRAIRIE, NEAR PALESTINE, TEXAS, AND WAS APPOINTED INDIAN AGENT FOR THE NACOGDOCHES AREA.

TWENTY YEARS LATER, IT WAS COL. BEAN WHO KEPT THE INDIANS *NEUTRAL* DURING THE TEXAS REVOLUTION.

BEAN MARRIED RICH AND DIED IN BED NEAR JALAPA, MEXICO IN 1846.

The Philip Nolan Filibuster

❶ Autumn 1800—Philip Nolan leads 28 heavily armed men into Texas on a northern route to evade Spanish patrols.

❷ Nolan's men build a log fort near the Brazos River in present-day Hill County.

❸ On March 21, 1801, a company of 120 Spanish soldiers make a surprise attack on Nolan's fort. Nolan is killed.

❹ Surviving filibusters are taken to Nacadoches, then

❺ to San Antonio.

❻ Eventually the filibusters are brought to a prison in Chihuahua, Mexico.

❼ The king decrees that for every five prisoners who had fired at Spanish troops at Nolan's fort, one would be executed. Since only nine prisoners fit that category, one would be executed.
On November 11 the Spaniards hang Ephriam Blackburn. The other men spend the rest of their lives in Mexico at hard labor.

❽ Only one prisoner, Ellis Bean, eventually escapes.

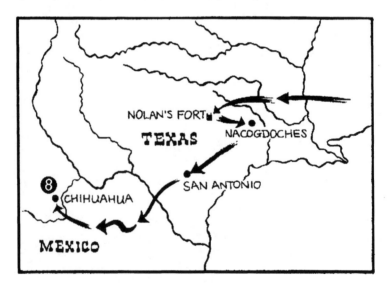

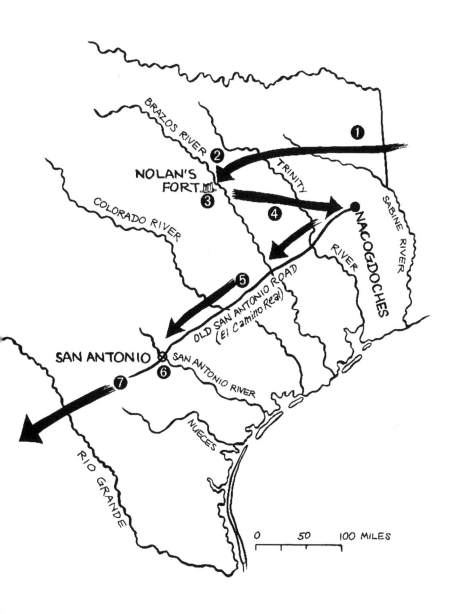

The Louisiana Purchase

CAUSED SOME TENSION BETWEEN THE UNITED STATES & SPAIN OVER THE OWNERSHIP OF TEXAS IN 1803. WHEN SELLING THE TERRITORY, THE FRENCH LED PRESIDENT THOMAS JEFFERSON TO BELIEVE HE WAS BUYING THE DEFUNCT FRENCH CLAIMS IN TEXAS.

UNITED STATES

LOUISIANA PURCHASE

TEXAS

Gulf of Mexico

JEFFERSON ADVISED THE SPANISH AMBASSADOR,

I EXPECT YOUR PEOPLE TO EVACUATE TEXAS!

SPAIN RESPONDED BY SENDING MORE TROOPS INTO EAST TEXAS AND STANDING FAST.

THE U.S. SENT A REVOLUTIONARY WAR VET, GEN. JAMES WILKINSON, TO LOUISIANA AND, IN 1806, HE OPENED PEACE TALKS WITH SPAIN'S GEN. SIMON HERRERA.

WITH NO AUTHORITY TO NEGOTIATE FOR THEIR COUNTRIES, GEN. JAMES WILKINSON OF THE U.S. & SPAIN'S GEN. SIMON HERRERA AGREED TO ESTABLISH A BUFFER ZONE BETWEEN THE SABINE RIVER AND THE ARROYO HONDO CREEK.

THE NEUTRAL GROUND,

AS IT WAS CALLED, SEPARATED THE LOUISIANA PURCHASE LANDS FROM THE SPANISH PROVINCE OF TEXAS IN 1806. FOR THE NEXT SIX YEARS THIS AREA WAS A HAVEN FOR THIEVES, KILLERS, SMUGGLERS, AND THE WORST DESPERADOS THE OLD BORDER HAD EVER KNOWN.

THE ENFORCER

WHEN LAW AND ORDER FINALLY DISINTEGRATED IN THE *NEUTRAL GROUND* IN 1810, THE U.S. ARMY SENT IN TROOPS TO GET RID OF THE TROUBLE-MAKERS. THE COMMANDER WAS A BRILLIANT BOSTON-IAN WHO GRADUATED THIRD IN HIS CLASS AT WEST POINT—**LIEUTENANT AUGUSTUS MAGEE.**

TO SHOW THAT THE UNITED STATES MEANT BUSINESS, LT. MAGEE HAD THE OUTLAWS HIS MEN CAPTURED TIED UP AND FLOGGED. SOON THE TROUBLE ENDED IN THE AREA.

DESPITE HIS GOOD RECORD, MAGEE WAS DENIED PROMOTION TO CAPTAIN. DISGUSTED, HE RESIGNED FROM THE ARMY IN 1812.

BACK IN LOUISIANA, MAGEE MET A REVOLUTIONARY GENERAL NAMED BERNARDO GUTIERREZ DE LARA WHO WAS TRYING TO RAISE AN ARMY TO OVERTHROW THE SPANISH RULERS OF MEXICO.

BERNARDO GUTIERREZ AND AUGUSTUS MAGEE PLANNED TO INVADE TEXAS AND LIBERATE IT FROM SPANISH RULE. WITH INDUCEMENTS OF $40 A MONTH AND A LEAGUE OF TEXAS LAND, MAGEE SOON ENLISTED A FEW HUNDRED AMERICANS, CAJUNS, MEXICANS, AND INDIANS IN WHAT HE CALLED

the Republican Army of the North.

IN AUGUST 1812 THE ARMY HEADED TO NACOGDOCHES, TEXAS.

REALIZING HE WAS HEAVILY OUTNUMBERED, CAPT. MONTERO, COMMANDER OF THE SPANISH GARRISON IN THE TOWN, ORDERED A RETREAT TO SAN ANTONIO.

WITHOUT FIRING A SHOT, THE FILIBUSTER (LAND PIRATE) ARMY TRIUMPHANTLY RODE INTO NACOGDOCHES.

The Magee-Gutierrez Expedition

LEFT NACOGDOCHES, MARCHED WEST, AND REACHED THE TRINITY RIVER IN OCTOBER 1812. THEY OCCUPIED A SPANISH VILLA, TRINIDAD DE SALCEDO, IN PRESENT-DAY MADISON COUNTY, DECLARED TEXAS A REPUBLIC, AND HOISTED A GREEN FLAG AS ITS EMBLEM.

THEIR NEXT OBJECTIVE WAS THE SPANISH STRONGHOLD OF BEXAR (SAN ANTONIO), BUT AS THEY WERE CROSSING THE COLORADO RIVER, A ROYALIST DESERTER WARNED MAGEE THAT GOVERNOR SALCEDO WAS WAITING WITH 1,400 TROOPS AT THE GUADALUPE RIVER.

The Siege of La Bahia

THE MAGEE-GUTIERREZ EXPEDITION BYPASSED GOVERNOR SALCEDO'S AMBUSH AND RODE 120 MILES TO LA BAHIA (NOW GOLIAD). CAUGHT OFF GUARD, THE 160 SPANISH DEFENDERS FLED IN TERROR. INSIDE, THE REVOLUTIONARIES FOUND THE SPANISH COMMISSARY AND PAYROLL.

AS MAGEE WAS PAYING HIS MEN WITH GOOD SILVER FROM THE SPANISH TREASURY, GOV. SALCEDO AND GEN. HERRERA SURROUNDED THE PLACE WITH 800 TROOPS. A FOUR MONTHS' SIEGE ENSUED.

COL. MAGEE DIED AT LA BAHIA (GOLIAD) IN FEB. 1813. SAM KEMPER TOOK HIS PLACE AS MILITARY COMMANDER OF THE MAGEE-GUTIERREZ EXPEDITION OF **FILIBUSTERS**—MEXICAN AND AMERICAN ADVENTURERS WHO TRIED TO LIBERATE TEXAS FROM THE SPANISH EMPIRE

IN MID-MARCH 1813, GOVERNOR SALCEDO LIFTED THE SIEGE ON LA BAHIA & RETREATED TO SAN ANTONIO

GUTIERREZ, KEMPER, AND 800 OF THEIR MEN FOLLOWED THE RETREATING SPANIARDS. ON MARCH 29, NINE MILES SOUTH OF SAN ANTONIO, KEMPER'S FILIBUSTERS RODE INTO AN

AMBUSH AT EL ROSILLO.

THE FILIBUSTERS CHARGED AND BROKE THROUGH THE SPANISH LINE, THEN PUSHED ON TO THE WALLS OF SAN ANTONIO.

Prelude to an Atrocity

APRIL 1, 1813—SAN ANTONIO WAS SURROUNDED BY 800 FILIBUSTERS UNDER KEMPER AND GUTIERREZ.
ON KEMPER'S PROMISE OF SAFE PASSAGE FOR THE SPANISH TROOPS, GOVERNOR SALCEDO SURRENDERED.

GUTIERREZ DECLARED HIMSELF PRESIDENT OF TEXAS, THEN HE OKAYED A **SECRET PLOT** BY CPT. ANTONIO DELGADO TO EXECUTE THE OFFICERS.

ON THE NIGHT OF APRIL 2, DELGADO LED ABOUT 100 REVOLU- TIONARIES TO THE PRISONERS' QUARTERS ON THE PLAZA AND ABDUCTED GOV. SALCEDO, GEN. HERRERA, AND 15 OTHER OFFICERS, AND MARCHED THEM OUT OF TOWN.

The Massacre at La Tablita

ON THE NIGHT OF APRIL 3, 1813 SOME 100 FILIBUSTERS (REBELS) UNDER ANTONIO DELGADO HERDED 17 SPANISH PRISONERS OF WAR, ALL OFFICERS, OUT OF SAN ANTONIO TO A PLACE CALLED *LA TABLITA*. HERE THEY TIED THE OFFICERS' HANDS AND...

CUT THEIR THROATS.

WHEN WORD ABOUT THE MASSACRE REACHED SAMUEL KEMPER, MILITARY COMMANDER OF THE FILIBUSTERS, HE IMMEDIATELY BROKE WITH "PRESIDENT" GUTIERREZ, THEN LED HUNDREDS OF VOLUNTEERS BACK TO THE UNITED STATES.

THE MASSACRE ALSO LED TO THE OUSTING OF GUTIERREZ AS "PRESIDENT" OF TEXAS. HE WENT BACK TO LOUISIANA.

ON AUGUST 4 GUTIERREZ WAS REPLACED BY JOSE ALVAREZ de TOLEDO.

Twilight of a Revolution

THE MAGEE-GUTIERREZ EXPEDITION BEGAN TO FALL APART IN AUG. 1813 WHEN HENRY PERRY TOOK OVER AS MILITARY COMMANDER AND JOSE TOLEDO BECAME "PRESIDENT" OF TEXAS. BOTH MEN INTENSELY HATED EACH OTHER.

MEANWHILE, JOAQUIN de ARREDONDO, COMMANDANT GENERAL OF NEW SPAIN'S EASTERN PROVINCES, LED A 2,000-MAN ARMY INTO TEXAS TO DRIVE OUT THE FILIBUSTERS.

ARREDONDO'S ARMY HALTED AT THE MEDINA RIVER. "PRESIDENT" TOLEDO WANTED TO DEFEND THE NORTH BANK AND MAKE THE SPANISH COME TO HIM, BUT PERRY REFUSED TO LISTEN.

HE STUBBORNLY LAUNCHED AN ALL-OUT ATTACK ACROSS THE MEDINA AT **LOSOYA.**

IT WAS EXACTLY WHAT ARREDONDO WANTED.

AUGUST 18, 1813—THE FILIBUSTER ARMY SPLASHED ACROSS THE MEDINA RIVER SOUTH OF SAN ANTONIO AT LOSOYA. THE SPANISH GENERAL ORDERED A FEW OF HIS COMPANIES TO FALL BACK AS IF IN A PANIC. THE AMERICAN, MEXICAN, AND INDIAN REVOLUTIONARIES GAVE CHASE AND QUICKLY FELL INTO

A TRAP.

GEN. ARREDONDO HAD SET UP A V-SHAPED AMBUSH. THE AMERICAN GROUP OF FILIBUSTERS UNDER HENRY PERRY STOOD AND FOUGHT UNTIL ALMOST ALL WERE KILLED.

THE MEXICANS AND INDIANS UNDER "PRES." TOLEDO TRIED TO ESCAPE TO LOUISIANA. ONLY A FEW MADE IT. THE REST WERE HUNTED DOWN AND KILLED.

THAT WAS THE END OF THE MAGEE-GUTIERREZ EXPEDITION.

Summary of the Magee-Gutierrez Expedition

❶ August 1812–Lieutenant Augustus Magee leads the Republic Army of the North into Texas and occupies Nacogdoches.

❷ October 1812–Magee's Army moves southward to take control of San Antonio de Bexar, capital of the province of Texas.

❸ Warned that Spanish forces are waiting for him at Bexar, Magee changes direction and

❹ attacks and overruns La Bahia.

❺ Spanish army attacks La Bahia. Siege lasts four months. Magee dies; Samuel Kemper replaces him as commander.

❻ February 1813–Republic Army leaves La Bahia and marches northward.

❼ Republic Army defeats Spanish at battle of El Rosillo, executes Spanish prisoners.

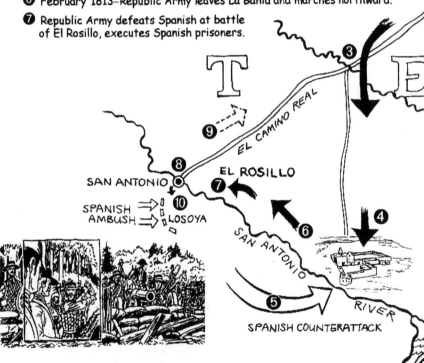

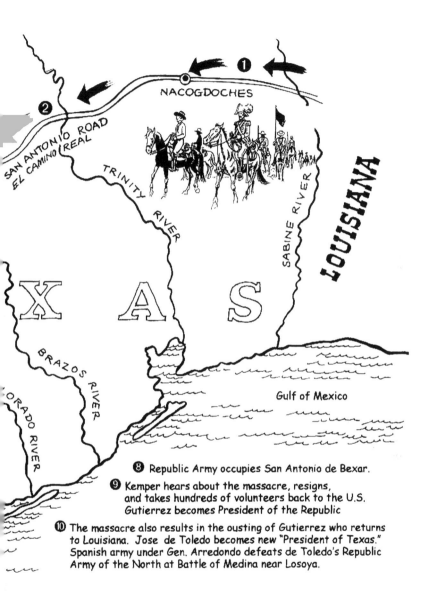

NACOGDOCHES

SAN ANTONIO ROAD
EL CAMINO REAL

TRINITY RIVER

SABINE RIVER

LOUISIANA

X A S

BRAZOS RIVER

ORADO RIVER

Gulf of Mexico

⑧ Republic Army occupies San Antonio de Bexar.

⑨ Kemper hears about the massacre, resigns,
and takes hundreds of volunteers back to the U.S.
Gutierrez becomes President of the Republic

⑩ The massacre also results in the ousting of Gutierrez who returns
to Louisiana. Jose de Toledo becomes new "President of Texas."
Spanish army under Gen. Arredondo defeats de Toledo's Republic
Army of the North at Battle of Medina near Losoya.

JEAN LAFITTE

WAS BORN IN BAYONNE, FRANCE AND EMIGRATED TO NEW ORLEANS WHERE HE WORKED IN A BLACKSMITH SHOP.

AROUND 1807 HE AND HIS BROTHER, PIERRE, COMMANDED A FLEET OF SHIPS THAT RAIDED SPANISH AND NEUTRAL VESSELS IN THE CARIBBEAN. THEIR SMUGGLING HEADQUARTERS WAS ON GRAND TERRE ISLAND IN BARATARIA BAY IN THE GULF OF MEXICO.

LAFITTE CONSIDERED HIMSELF A LOYAL AMERICAN. DURING THE WAR OF 1812 HE SUPPLIED GEN. ANDY JACKSON WITH TONS OF WEAPONS AND AMMUNITION ALONG WITH HIS PIRATES TO FIGHT THE BRITISH AT THE BATTLE OF NEW ORLEANS.

FOR THIS, JEAN AND PIERRE GOT A PRESIDENTIAL PARDON. IN 1816 THE LAFITTES AND THEIR CREW RELOCATED TO TEXAS.

LOUIS-MICHEL **AURY** WAS A FRENCH PRIVATEER RAIDING AND PLUNDERING IN THE CARIBBEAN SEA.

MEXICAN REBELS HIRED HIM AND, ON JUNE 17, 1816, AURY'S FLEET BLASTED ITS WAY INTO THE NEW SPAIN PORT OF **GALVESTON, TEXAS.**

JOSE MANUEL de HERRERA PROCLAIMED GALVESTON AS A PORT OF THE MEXICAN REPUBLIC AND APPOINTED AURY AS THE RESIDENT COMMISSIONER.

MEANWHILE, ANOTHER PIRATE, JEAN LAFITTE, WAS HIRED BY THE SPANISH TO GO AFTER AURY.

License to Steal

LOUIS-MICHEL AURY WAS THE RESIDENT COMMISSIONER OF THE GALVESTON PORT UNDER THE REBEL GOVERNMENT OF MEXICO IN 1816. HE CONSIDERED THIS A LICENSE TO STEAL. HIS PRIVATEER FLEET CRUISED THE GULF OF MEXICO LOOKING FOR MERCHANT SHIPS TO RAID AND PLUNDER.

AURY'S HEADQUARTERS WAS A CLUSTER OF SHACKS ON GALVESTON ISLAND.

IN NOVEMBER 1816, FRANCISCO XAVIER MINA, THE SPANISH REBEL, DROPPED IN ON AURY TO SEEK HIS HELP IN ATTACKING MEXICO.

FRANCISCO XAVIER MINA

PLANNED TO INVADE MEXICO TO OVERTHROW ITS SPANISH GOVERNMENT. GEN. WINFIELD SCOTT HAD LED HIM TO BELIEVE THAT THE UNITED STATES WOULD SEND HIM REINFORCEMENTS.

IN LATE 1816 MINA WENT TO GALVESTON, TEXAS TO SEEK NAVAL SUPPORT FROM LOUIS-MICHEL AURY, THE PIRATE.

THEY SAILED ON APRIL 7, 1817. AURY COMMANDED THE FLEET OF EIGHT SHIPS, WHILE MINA TOOK CHARGE OF THE 235 INFANTRYMEN.

THEY GOT TO MEXICO ON APRIL 11.

MINA'S MEN RUSHED ASHORE AND WON A FEW SKIRMISHES AGAINST THE SPANISH

U.S. HELP WAS NOWHERE IN SIGHT.

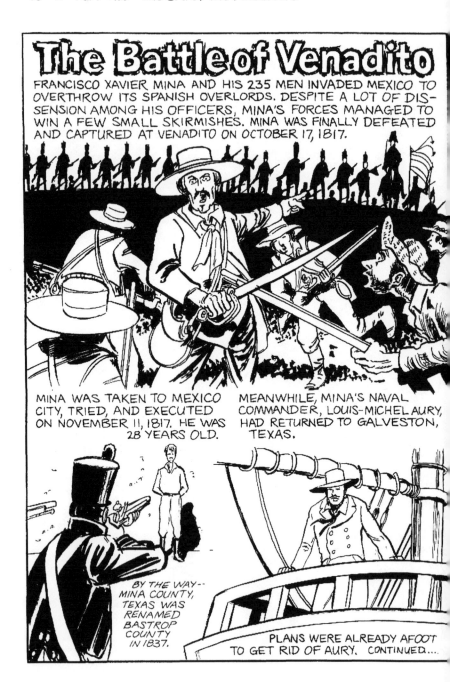

The Battle of Venadito

FRANCISCO XAVIER MINA AND HIS 235 MEN INVADED MEXICO TO OVERTHROW ITS SPANISH OVERLORDS. DESPITE A LOT OF DISSENSION AMONG HIS OFFICERS, MINA'S FORCES MANAGED TO WIN A FEW SMALL SKIRMISHES. MINA WAS FINALLY DEFEATED AND CAPTURED AT VENADITO ON OCTOBER 17, 1817.

MINA WAS TAKEN TO MEXICO CITY, TRIED, AND EXECUTED ON NOVEMBER 11, 1817. HE WAS 28 YEARS OLD.

MEANWHILE, MINA'S NAVAL COMMANDER, LOUIS-MICHEL AURY, HAD RETURNED TO GALVESTON, TEXAS.

BY THE WAY-- MINA COUNTY, TEXAS WAS RENAMED BASTROP COUNTY IN 1837.

PLANS WERE ALREADY AFOOT TO GET RID OF AURY. CONTINUED....

Getting Rid of Aury

LOUIS-MICHEL AURY WAS PLUNDERING SHIPS ON THE CARIBBEAN AND HELPING MEXICAN REVOLUTIONARIES. THE SPANISH RULERS OF MEXICO DECIDED TO *NEUTRALIZE* THE PIRATE. TO ACCOMPLISH THIS THEY HIRED OTHER PIRATES AS *SECRET AGENTS*, NAMELY, THE LAFITTE BROTHERS—JEAN AND PIERRE.

WHILE AURY WAS AWAY ON THE MINA EXPEDITION, THE LAFITTES LEFT LOUISIANA AND SAILED TO HIS HEADQUARTERS AT GALVESTON, TEXAS.

WITHIN A FEW WEEKS THEY CONVINCED AURY'S MEN TO JOIN THE LAFITTE GANG

AURY RETURNED TO GALVESTON IN JUNE 1817 ONLY TO FIND HIS POWER USURPED. HE LEFT TEXAS FOR GOOD A MONTH LATER.

AURY DIED IN 1821.

JEAN LAFITTE CALLED HIS FIEFDOM ON GALVESTON ISLAND *THE REPUBLIC OF MEXICO.* YET, HE CONSIDERED HIMSELF A LOYAL AMERICAN. THAT IS WHY HE WAS QUITE ANNOYED WHEN U.S. NEWSPAPERS, DESCRIBING HIS EXPLOITS ON THE SPANISH MAIN, LABELED HIM THE

PIRATE OF THE GULF.

ON ONE RAID LAFITTE ROBBED A GOLD CHAIN AND THE CHURCH SEAL FROM A BISHOP WHO WAS ON A PILGRIMAGE TO ROME.

THIS LOOT WAS GIVEN TO REZIN BOWIE A COLLAB- ORATOR WITH LAFITTE IN THE SLAVE TRADING RACKET.

The Ultimatum

JEAN LAFITTE GAVE STRICT ORDERS TO HIS CAPTAINS NOT TO HARASS UNITED STATES SHIPS. BUT, WHEN ONE OF HIS PRIVATEERS ATTACKED AN AMERICAN MERCHANT VESSEL, PRESIDENT JAMES MONROE DECIDED THAT THE LAFITTE GANG HAD TO GO. HE SENT THE NAVY TO TEXAS.

BANG BOOM BLAST

A SQUADRON OF U.S. FRIGATES SAILED INTO GALVESTON BAY. THE SKIPPER GAVE THE LAFITTES UNTIL MAY 21, 1820 TO "LEAVE OR ELSE."

THE FALL OF LAFITTE

THE U.S. NAVY GAVE JEAN LAFITTE AND HIS PIRATES UNTIL MAY 21, 1820 TO LEAVE GALVESTON ISLAND OR BE BLOWN AWAY.

LAFITTE BROKE OUT HIS VAST LIQUOR STORES AND THREW A GALA PARTY FOR HIS FOLLOWERS.

THEN HE TORCHED THE TOWN OF CAMPEACHY (HIS HEADQUARTERS) AND LEFT FOR PARTS UNKNOWN, SOME BELIEVE TO THE YUCATAN.

HE CONTINUED HIS ILLEGAL ESCAPADES UNTIL 1826 WHEN, MORTALLY ILL, HE LANDED ON AN UNKNOWN SHORE AND DIED.

FACING CHAOS IN FLORIDA, SPAIN DECIDED TO SELL THE COL-
ONY TO THE UNITED STATES FOR **FIVE MILLION DOLLARS.**
NEGOTIATED BY SPAIN'S AMBASSADOR TO THE U.S., LUIS de ONIS,
AND SECRETARY OF STATE JOHN QUINCY ADAMS, THE
AGREEMENT WAS KNOWN AS

THE ADAMS-ONIS TREATY.

THE TREATY HAD STRINGS ATTACHED: SPAIN WOULD
FORFEIT ALL CLAIMS TO THE OREGON TERRITORY WHILE THE
U.S. ABANDONED ITS SHADOWY CLAIM TO TEXAS.
THIS REALLY IRKED
SPECULATORS NEAR
THE TEXAS FRONTIER.

OCCUPIED JOINTLY BY THE U.S. AND GREAT BRITAIN

OREGON TERRITORY

LOUISIANA PURCHASE

THE UNITED STATES IN 1819.

MEXICO

TEXAS

(THE ADAMS-ONIS TREATY)

FLORIDA

IF THE U.S. WON'T CLAIM TEXAS,
WE'LL TAKE IT FOR OURSELVES!

THE U.S. GAVE UP ITS CLAIM ON TEXAS WITH THE ADAMS-ONIS TREATY IN 1819. QUICKLY A GROUP OF SPECULATORS AND MERCHANTS IN **NATCHEZ**, MISSISSIPPI PLOTTED TO TAKE CONTROL OF TEXAS FOR THEMSELVES. THEY STARTED BY RECRUITING A

FILIBUSTER* ARMY.

✻ AN OLD-FASHIONED TERM FOR A MERCENARY, OR A "LAND PIRATE."

WE HAVE RAISED A HALF MILLION DOLLARS TO FIELD AN ARMY.

AMONG THE RINGLEADERS WAS BERNARDO GUTIERREZ WHO HAD LED AN ILL-FATED FILIBUSTER EXPEDITION TO TEXAS IN 1813.

EACH SOLDIER WILL GET ONE LEAGUE OF LAND IN TEXAS.

OUR COMMANDING GENERAL IS DOCTOR **JAMES LONG.**

Another Republic of Texas

DR. (AND GENERAL) **JAMES LONG** LEFT NATCHEZ, MISSISSIPPI WITH A FORCE OF EIGHTY MEN AND HEADED FOR TEXAS IN JUNE 1819.

SOON HE HAD 300 TROOPERS.

AT THE TIME NACOGDOCHES WAS THE ONLY SIZEABLE TOWN IN EAST TEXAS, BUT IT WAS ALMOST DESERTED AS THE RESULT OF A RECENT REBELLION.

LONG'S MEN EASILY TOOK OVER THE TOWN AND CONVENED A **SUPREME COUNCIL** ON JUNE 23rd.

WE DECLARE TEXAS AN INDEPENDENT REPUBLIC AND DR. LONG AS OUR **PRESIDENT!**

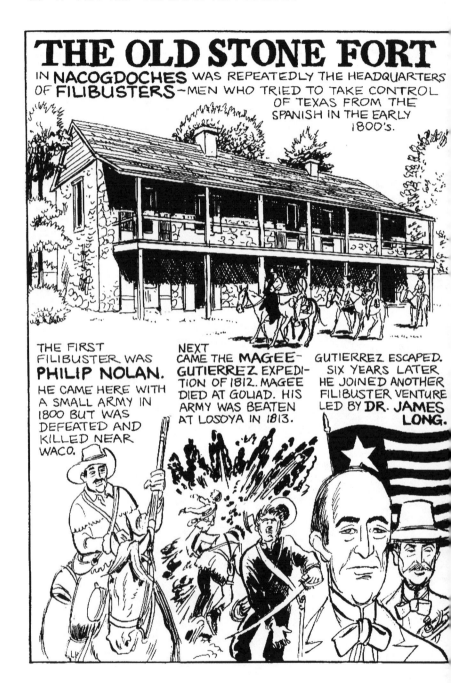

THE OLD STONE FORT

IN **NACOGDOCHES** WAS REPEATEDLY THE HEADQUARTERS OF **FILIBUSTERS**—MEN WHO TRIED TO TAKE CONTROL OF TEXAS FROM THE SPANISH IN THE EARLY 1800's.

THE FIRST FILIBUSTER WAS **PHILIP NOLAN.**

HE CAME HERE WITH A SMALL ARMY IN 1800 BUT WAS DEFEATED AND KILLED NEAR WACO.

NEXT CAME THE **MAGEE-GUTIERREZ** EXPEDITION OF 1812. MAGEE DIED AT GOLIAD. HIS ARMY WAS BEATEN AT LOSOYA IN 1813.

GUTIERREZ ESCAPED. SIX YEARS LATER HE JOINED ANOTHER FILIBUSTER VENTURE LED BY **DR. JAMES LONG.**

Filibuster Trading Posts

DR. JAMES LONG WAS THE FIRST FILIBUSTER LEADER TO PROMOTE COMMERCE IN TEXAS. IN 1819 HE SENT OUT AGENTS TO SET UP TRADING POSTS TO DO BUSINESS WITH THE NATIVES.

THESE TRADING POSTS WERE LOCATED ON THE TRINITY RIVER CROSSING, THE FALLS ON THE BRAZOS, PECAN POINT ON THE RED RIVER, COUSHATTA VILLAGE NEAR PRESENT DAY LIVINGSTON, AND LA BAHIA CROSSING NEAR WHAT IS NOW WASHINGTON.

Knocking Off the Filibusters

THE SPANISH GOVERNMENT QUICKLY REACTED TO THE ATTEMPTED TAKEOVER OF TEXAS BY DR. JAMES LONG AND HIS FILIBUSTERS. THEY SENT 550 TROOPS TO STOP THE INCURSION IN SEPTEMBER 1819.

THEY WERE COMMANDED BY COLONEL IGNACIO PEREZ.

PEREZ HIT THE FRINGES OF THE FILIBUSTERS' REPUBLIC AND STARTED TO KNOCK OFF THEIR TRADING POSTS AT THE FALLS ON THE BRAZOS AND LA BAHIA CROSSING.

DR. LONG'S BROTHER WAS KILLED.

Collapse of the Republic

COLONEL IGNACIO PEREZ LED A BRIGADE OF 550 SPANISH SOLDIERS FROM SAN ANTONIO ON A CAMPAIGN TO ROUT JAMES LONG'S FILIBUSTERS. EARLY IN OCTOBER 1819 THEY OBLITERATED THE FILIBUSTER TRADING POST ON THE TRINITY RIVER.

ON OCTOBER 28 THE SPANIARDS OVERRAN NACOGDOCHES, THE CAPITAL OF LONG'S REPUBLIC OF TEXAS.

UNAWARE OF ALL THIS, DR. LONG, PRESIDENT OF THE REPUBLIC, WAS WENDING HIS WAY TO NACOGDOCHES FOLLOWING HIS DISAPPOINTING MEETING WITH JEAN LAFITTE IN GALVESTON.

Escape Across the Sabine

MID-OCTOBER 1819—COLONEL IGNACIO PEREZ SPLIT HIS SPAN-ISH BRIGADE. HE PERSONALLY LED ONE BATTALION TO SMASH THE FILIBUSTER TRADING CENTER AT THE COUSHATTA VILLAGE IN PRESENT-DAY POLK COUNTY.

THE OTHER FORCE WENT AFTER DR. JAMES LONG'S HEADQUARTERS IN NACOGDOCHES FOREWARNED, THE FILIBUSTERS RACED EASTWARD AND CROSSED THE SABINE RIVER INTO LOUISIANA.

MEANWHILE THE FILIBUSTERS' LEADER, DR. JAMES LONG, WAS UNAWARE OF THIS CRISIS.

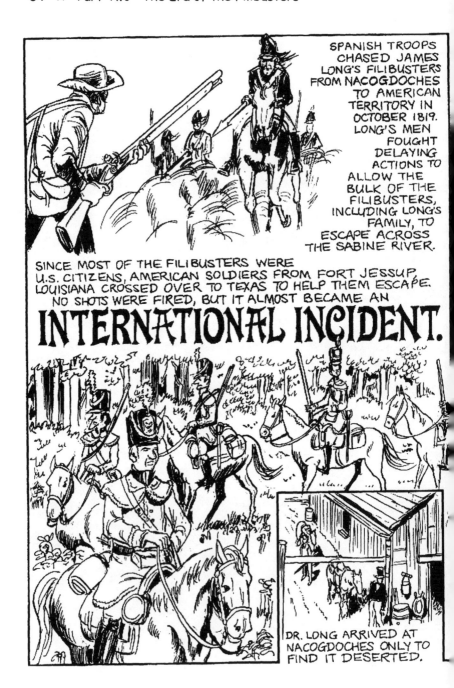

SPANISH TROOPS CHASED JAMES LONG'S FILIBUSTERS FROM NACOGDOCHES TO AMERICAN TERRITORY IN OCTOBER 1819. LONG'S MEN FOUGHT DELAYING ACTIONS TO ALLOW THE BULK OF THE FILIBUSTERS, INCLUDING LONG'S FAMILY, TO ESCAPE ACROSS THE SABINE RIVER.

SINCE MOST OF THE FILIBUSTERS WERE U.S. CITIZENS, AMERICAN SOLDIERS FROM FORT JESSUP, LOUISIANA CROSSED OVER TO TEXAS TO HELP THEM ESCAPE. NO SHOTS WERE FIRED, BUT IT ALMOST BECAME AN

INTERNATIONAL INCIDENT.

DR. LONG ARRIVED AT NACOGDOCHES ONLY TO FIND IT DESERTED.

A SPANISH BRIGADE DROVE MOST OF JAMES LONG'S FILIBUSTERS OUT OF TEXAS IN OCTOBER 1819. DR. LONG AND REMNANTS OF HIS FOLLOWERS HIGH-TAILED IT TO GALVESTON. THERE, ON BOLIVAR POINT AT THE EASTERN TIP OF THE ISLAND, THEY BUILT **FORT LAS CASAS.**

WEEKS WENT BY AND NOTHING HAPPENED.

EVENTUALLY DR. LONG REALIZED THAT HIS *REPUBLIC OF TEXAS* WAS NO MORE.

FINALLY HE WENT BACK TO LOUISIANA WITH DREAMS OF STARTING OVER.

JANE WILKINSON

WAS BORN IN CHARLES COUNTY, MARYLAND ON JULY 23, 1798. AFTER HER FATHER DIED, SHE MOVED WITH HER MOTHER TO NATCHEZ, MISSISSIPPI. A CHANCE MEETING AND A WHIRL-WIND COURTSHIP LED TO HER MARRIAGE TO **DOCTOR JAMES LONG** ON MAY 14, 1815.

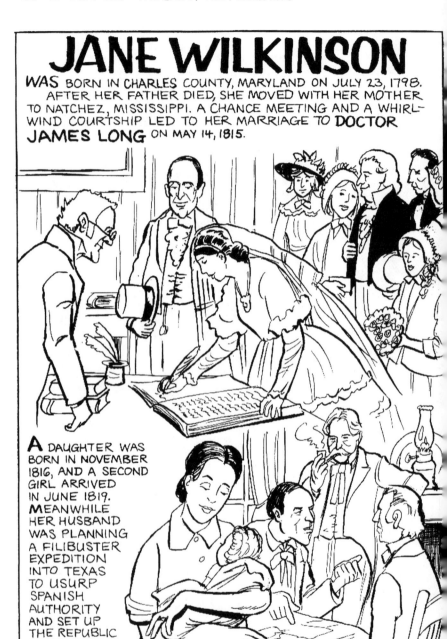

A DAUGHTER WAS BORN IN NOVEMBER 1816, AND A SECOND GIRL ARRIVED IN JUNE 1819. MEANWHILE HER HUSBAND WAS PLANNING A FILIBUSTER EXPEDITION INTO TEXAS TO USURP SPANISH AUTHORITY AND SET UP THE REPUBLIC OF TEXAS.

DR. JAMES LONG LEFT NATCHEZ, MISSISSIPPI IN JUNE 1819 ON A FILIBUSTER EXPEDITION INTO TEXAS. HIS WIFE, **JANE LONG,** PROCEEDED TO JOIN HIM A FEW WEEKS LATER. ACCOMPANIED BY HER DAUGHTERS AND A GOVERNESS NAMED KIAMATIA, JANE BOOKED PASSAGE ON A BOAT HEADING UP THE RED RIVER.

ALONG THE WAY JANE TOOK SICK AND HAD TO SUFFER ON BOARD UNTIL THE BOAT REACHED ALEXANDRIA, LOUISIANA, THE HOME OF HER SISTER, MRS. ALEXANDER CALVIT.

SHE STAYED WITH HER SISTER FOR TWO WEEKS, THEN RESUMED HER TRIP TO TEXAS.

JANE'S BABY WAS IN ILL HEALTH, SO SHE WAS LEFT WITH MRS. CALVIT.

Reunited...briefly

JANE LONG CAUGHT UP WITH HER HUSBAND AT NACOGDOCHES, TEXAS IN LATE SUMMER 1819.

DR. LONG, BY THEN PRESIDENT OF THE REPUBLIC OF TEXAS, WAS PREOCCUPIED WITH RUNNING HIS REVOLUTIONARY GOVERNMENT AND WORRIED ABOUT AN ATTACK BY SPANISH FORCES.

IN SEPTEMBER, DR. LONG DEPARTED FOR GALVESTON TO MEET WITH LAFITTE.

JANE AND HER LITTLE GIRL WERE LEFT IN NACOGDOCHES TO FEND FOR THEMSELVES.

Long's Second Attempt

DR. JAMES LONG'S REPUBLIC OF TEXAS WENT UP IN FLAMES IN 1819, BUT HE VOWED TO START OVER. HE RETURNED TO LOUISIANA TO PICK UP HIS WIFE, DAUGHTER, AND THEIR SERVANT, THEN SAILED TO HIS FORT AT BOLIVAR POINT ON GALVESTON ISLAND.

ON APRIL 6, 1820, LONG ARRIVED AT BOLIVAR POINT WHERE SOME OF HIS REVOLUTIONARIES WERE STAYING. HE PROMPTLY ANNOUNCED HIS INTENTION TO START ANOTHER REVOLUTION IN TEXAS.

ALL MEMBERS OF THE FORMER REPUBLIC MUST REPORT HERE NO LATER THAN APRIL TENTH.

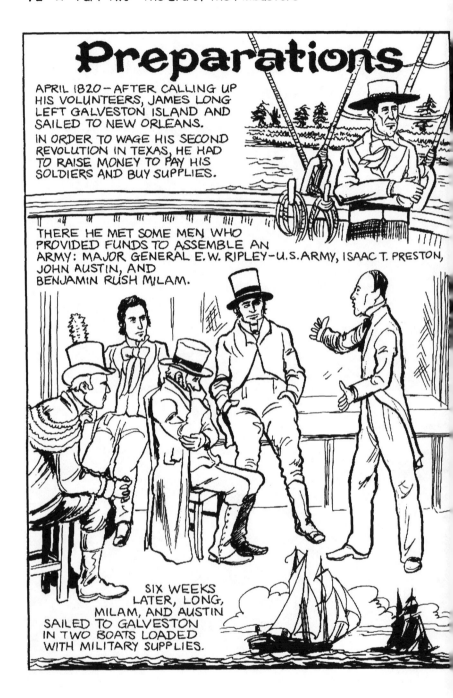

Preparations

APRIL 1820—AFTER CALLING UP HIS VOLUNTEERS, JAMES LONG LEFT GALVESTON ISLAND AND SAILED TO NEW ORLEANS.

IN ORDER TO WAGE HIS SECOND REVOLUTION IN TEXAS, HE HAD TO RAISE MONEY TO PAY HIS SOLDIERS AND BUY SUPPLIES.

THERE HE MET SOME MEN WHO PROVIDED FUNDS TO ASSEMBLE AN ARMY: MAJOR GENERAL E. W. RIPLEY—U.S. ARMY, ISAAC T. PRESTON, JOHN AUSTIN, AND BENJAMIN RUSH MILAM.

SIX WEEKS LATER, LONG, MILAM, AND AUSTIN SAILED TO GALVESTON IN TWO BOATS LOADED WITH MILITARY SUPPLIES.

The President Without a Country

DR. JAMES LONG, JOHN AUSTIN, AND BEN MILAM ARRIVED AT GALVESTON ISLAND WITH SUPPLIES TO START ANOTHER REVOLUTION IN TEXAS. LONG CONVENED THE SUPREME COUNCIL ON JUNE 4, 1820 AT FORT LAS CASAS. THEY ELECTED MAJOR GENERAL ELEAZER WHEELOCK RIPLEY **PRESIDENT** OF THE REPUBLIC OF TEXAS.

I WILL WRITE TO GENERAL RIPLEY IN NEW ORLEANS AND OFFER HIM A YEARLY SALARY OF $25,000 AND TWENTY MILES OF LAND.

GENERAL RIPLEY WAS A DARTMOUTH GRADUATE AND HERO OF THE WAR OF 1812.

ALTHOUGH THE REPUBLIC DID NOT HAVE 25 CENTS, RIPLEY ACCEPTED THE JOB BUT NEVER CAME TO TEXAS.

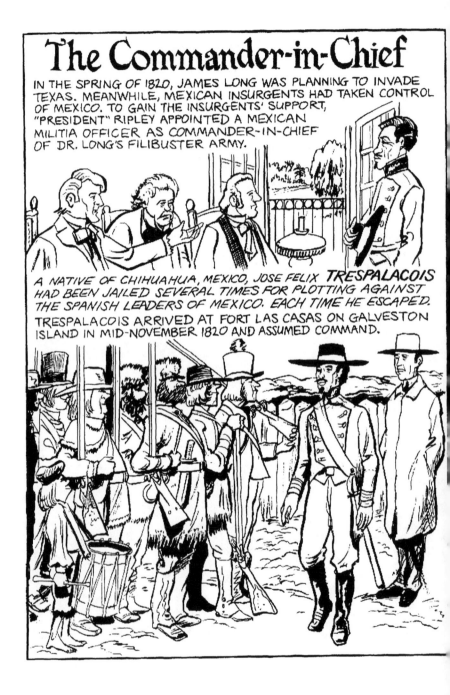

The Commander-in-Chief

IN THE SPRING OF 1820, JAMES LONG WAS PLANNING TO INVADE TEXAS. MEANWHILE, MEXICAN INSURGENTS HAD TAKEN CONTROL OF MEXICO. TO GAIN THE INSURGENTS' SUPPORT, "PRESIDENT" RIPLEY APPOINTED A MEXICAN MILITIA OFFICER AS COMMANDER-IN-CHIEF OF DR. LONG'S FILIBUSTER ARMY.

A NATIVE OF CHIHUAHUA, MEXICO, JOSE FELIX *TRESPALACOIS* HAD BEEN JAILED SEVERAL TIMES FOR PLOTTING AGAINST THE SPANISH LEADERS OF MEXICO. EACH TIME HE ESCAPED.

TRESPALACOIS ARRIVED AT FORT LAS CASAS ON GALVESTON ISLAND IN MID-NOVEMBER 1820 AND ASSUMED COMMAND.

DR. JAMES LONG'S EXPEDITION TO TAKE CONTROL OF TEXAS HIT A SNAG WHEN THE TREASURY NOTES THAT WERE TO PAY HIS SOLDIERS PROVED TO BE WORTHLESS. THIS RESULTED IN

A SLIGHT CASE OF MUTINY.

COMMANDANTÉ TRESPALACOIS DECIDED TO RETURN TO NEW ORLEANS IN LATE 1820 TO STRAIGHTEN OUT THE MESS. ABOUT FIFTY MALCONTENTS WENT WITH HIM.

MEANWHILE, **MOSES AUSTIN** WAS IN **SAN ANTONIO** TRYING TO GET PERMISSION TO SET UP HIS OWN COLONY IN TEXAS. FAMILIAR WITH LONG'S SITUATION, AUSTIN TOLD GOVERNOR MARTINEZ,

LONG HAS BEEN ABANDONED BY ALL BUT THIRTY MEN, AND AMERICAN SENTIMENT IS AGAINST HIM.

I DO NOT FEAR DR. LONG'S ARMY. HE WILL BE DEALT WITH WHEN THE TIME COMES.

THE LAST FILIBUSTER

FINALLY GOT UNDER WAY ON SEPTEMBER 19, 1821 WHEN DR. JAMES LONG'S FILIBUSTER ARMY OF ABOUT 52 MEN LEFT LAS CASAS ON GALVESTON IS. AND SAILED SOUTH.

THEY LANDED AT SAN ANTONIO BAY AND MARCHED INLAND. THEIR STRATEGY WAS TO LAUNCH A NIGHT ATTACK ON LA BAHIA, THE EASTERNMOST PRESIDIO IN TEXAS.

IF SUCCESSFUL, DR. LONG AND COMMANDANTE TRESPALACIOS BELIEVED GOVERNOR MARTINEZ WOULD BE FORCED TO NEGOTIATE AND JOIN THE REPUBLIC OF TEXAS.

The Taking of La Bahia

FRANCISCO GARCIA, COMMANDER OF LA BAHIA, HAD NO CLUE THAT HIS PRESIDIO WAS ABOUT TO BE ATTACKED. SO, ON THE NIGHT OF OCTOBER 6, 1821, HE DID NOT POST SENTRIES.

COMMANDANTÉ TRESPALACIOS, DR. JAMES LONG, AND THEIR ARMY OF 52 MEN SIMPLY WALKED IN AND TOOK POSSESSION.

IMMEDIATELY DR. LONG WROTE TO GOVERNOR MARTINEZ IN SAN ANTONIO REQUESTING A CONFERENCE.

Emperor Augustin I

MEXICAN FORCES CAPTURED JAMES LONG AND HIS FILIBUSTER ARMY AT LA BAHIA ON OCTOBER 8, 1821.

THEY WERE TAKEN TO SAN ANTONIO THEN EVENTUALLY TO MEXICO CITY.

FOR MONTHS DR. LONG LANGUISHED IN A MEXICO CITY JAIL.

MEANWHILE, AUGUSTIN de **ITURBIDE**, A ROYALIST OFFICER IN MEXICO, BETRAYED THE SPANISH, KICKED OUT THE VICEROY, AND DECLARED HIMSELF AUGUSTIN THE FIRST— **EMPEROR OF MEXICO.** WHEN DR. LONG HEARD ABOUT THIS...

I DEMAND TO MEET WITH ITURBIDE!

MY EXPEDITION WAS PART OF A LARGE EFFORT TO FREE MEXICO FROM SPAIN.

SHE WHO WAITS

WHEN DR. JAMES LONG LEFT GALVESTON ISLAND IN SEPTEMBER 1821 TO ATTACK LA BAHIA, HE LEFT HIS WIFE, DAUGHTER, AND THEIR SERVANT AT FORT LAS CASAS.

MANNING THE FORT WAS A HANDFUL OF SOLDIERS.

MRS. LONG, THE KARANKAWAS COULD OVERRUN THE FORT ANYTIME.

PLEASE LEAVE WITH US NOW!

I SHALL REMAIN HERE UNTIL MY HUSBAND RETURNS.

THE SOLDIERS DEPARTED. EVEN THOUGH SHE WAS PREGNANT, MRS. JANE LONG STAYED AT FORT LAS CASAS, ACCOMPA-NIED ONLY BY HER DAUGHTER AND KIAMATA, THEIR SERVANT.

Summary of the
James Long Filibuster, 1819-1822

❶ Dr. James Long and 300 men enter Texas in June 1819. These filubusters occupy Nacagdoches, declare Texas an independent Republic, and vote Long its president.

❷ Long sends out agents to set up trading posts.

❸ Long goes to Galveston to seek the aid of Jean Lafitte.

❹ In September 1891, Spanish forces under Col. Ignacio Perez attack Long's trading posts on the Brazos and La Bahia crossing.

❺ Spaniards overrun Nacagdoches and pursue Long's men into Louisiana.

❻ Dr. Long retreats to Bolivar Point on Galveston Island and builds Fort Las Casas. He stays here for months trying to figure out what to do next.

❼ By September 1821 Long has organized another filibuster expedition and they leave Las Casas, sail to Matagorda, and

❽ march overland to La Bahia.

SAN ANTONIO

LA BAHIA

❾ On October 6, 1821, Long's men attack La Bahia and take over the presidio.

❿ Two days later Col. Perez's troops counterattack La Bahia. Long's men surrender. He is taken to Mexico where he is assassinated on April 8, 1822.

DING
ST AT
NITY
SSING

NACOGDOCHES

RADING
POSTS

TRINITY RIVER

X A S

LOUISIANA

SABINE RIVER

BRAZOS RIVER

BOLIVAR POINT

GALVESTON ISLAND

MATAGORDA

Gulf of Mexico

Standoff at Bolivar Point

SEVERAL TIMES DURING NOVEMBER AND DECEMBER 1821 GROUPS OF KARANKAWA INDIANS STARTED TO ATTACK FORT LAS CASAS AT BOLIVAR POINT ON GALVESTON ISLAND.

ALONE ON GALVESTON ISLAND WITH HER DAUGHTER, ANN, AND SERVANT, MRS. JANE LONG GAVE BIRTH TO ANOTHER DAUGHTER, MARY, ON DECEMBER 21, 1821. SINCE THIS WAS THE FIRST RECORDED BIRTH OF AN ANGLO IN TEXAS, JANE LONG BECAME KNOWN AS

THE MOTHER OF TEXAS.

FIVE DAYS LATER A LETTER FROM HER HUSBAND WAS BROUGHT FROM MONTERREY, MEXICO.

JAMES HAS BEEN CAPTURED AND IS BEING TAKEN TO PRISON IN MEXICO CITY. OUR CAUSE IS LOST.

JANE, HER DAUGHTERS, AND SERVANT LEFT GALVESTON IN JANUARY 1822 AND WENT TO LIVE WITH THE SMITH FAMILY ON THE BRAZOS IN A CABIN BUILT FOR HER BY DR. LONG'S FOLLOWERS.

"WE REGRET TO INFORM YOU..."

MRS. JANE LONG WAS LIVING IN A CABIN ON THE BRAZOS IN JULY 1822 WHEN RANDALL AND JAMES W. JONES RODE UP AND INFORMED HER THAT HER HUSBAND, JAMES, HAD DIED THREE MONTHS AGO IN A MEXICO CITY PRISON.

EVENTUALLY BEN MILAM BROUGHT JANE HER HUSBAND'S BLOOD-STAINED CLOTHES AND TOLD HER HOW DR. LONG WAS KILLED

AROUND SEPTEMBER 1822, MRS. LONG ACCEPTED AN INVITATION BY THE NEW GOVERNOR OF THE MEXICAN PROVINCE OF TEXAS TO MOVE TO SAN ANTONIO.

THAT GOVERNOR WAS COL. JOSE FELIX TRESPALACOIS, FORMER COMMANDANT OF DR. JAMES LONG'S FILIBUSTER ARMY.

Baby Mary Long

JANE LONG LIVED BRIEFLY IN SAN ANTONIO IN 1823.

THEN SHE WENT BACK TO NATCHEZ, MISSISSIPPI AND STAYED WITH HER SISTER AND BROTHER-IN-LAW, ALEXANDER CALVIT.

EARLY IN 1824 JANE CONVINCED THE CALVITS TO MOVE TO TEXAS WITH HER AS PART OF STEPHEN F. **AUSTIN'S THREE HUNDRED.**

THE CONSTANT TRAVELING, HARSH CONDITIONS, AND POOR NUTRITION TOOK ITS TOLL ON JANE'S TEXAS-BORN BABY, MARY.

THE 18 MONTH-OLD CHILD DIED IN JUNE 1824.

Jane's Boarding Houses

JANE LONG LIVED IN SAN FELIPE FOR A FEW YEARS. THEN, FROM 1834 TO THE 1840s, JANE AND HER SERVANT, KIAMATA, OPERATED BOARDING HOUSES, FIRST IN **BRAZORIA**, THEN IN **RICHMOND**. THEIR GUESTS INCLUDED A WHO'S WHO OF PROMINENT TEXANS OF THE COLONY AND THE REPUBLIC.

WHILE RUNNING THESE HOSTELRIES MRS. LONG PROMOTED HERSELF AS *THE MOTHER OF TEXAS.*

SHE TOLD AND RETOLD THE STORY OF HER HUSBAND'S FILIBUSTER EXPEDITIONS OF 1819 AND 1821, AND HOW SHE GAVE BIRTH IN THE MIDDLE OF WINTER AT BOLIVAR POINT.

Jane's Plantation

JANE LONG HAD PURCHASED 50,000 ACRES IN FORT BEND COUNTY IN 1837. TO EARN A LIVING SHE RAN A BOARDING HOUSE ON 4th ST. IN RICHMOND. WHEN HER **OLD SOUTH PLANTATION** BECAME PROFITABLE IN THE 1840s, JANE MOVED THERE PERMANENTLY.

THE MUSEUM OF SOUTHERN HISTORY ON FM 359, NORTH OF RICHMOND, NOW OCCUPIES TEN ACRES OF JANE'S PLANTATION.

HER SURVIVING DAUGHTER, ANN MARRIED THE HON. JAMES S. SULLIVAN OF RICHMOND.

MRS. JANE LONG, *THE MOTHER OF TEXAS*, DIED IN 1880 AT AGE 82 AND WAS BURIED IN RICHMOND'S MORTON CEMETERY.

KIAMATA, NICKNAMED KIAN, REMAINED A SERVANT AND FRIEND OF MRS. JANE LONG ALL HER LIFE.

MRS. LONG AND KIAN DID ALL THE MENIAL CHORES AT JANE'S BOARDING-HOUSE—NOW PRESERVED AT THE FORT BEND COUNTY MUSEUM IN RICHMOND.

KIAN HAD FOUR CHILDREN, TWO BOYS AND TWO GIRLS.

IT IS NOT KNOWN WHEN KIAN DIED.

ONE OF KIAN'S SONS, JIM LONG, WAS NAMED IN HONOR OF MRS. LONG'S HUSBAND. JIM WAS AN OVERSEER ON THE LONG PLANTATION. HE DIED IN SAN ANTONIO IN THE 1890s.

AROUND THAT TIME, THE LONG MANSION, SHOWN HERE, BURNED DOWN.

Part Three

The Era of the Empresarios
1824 to 1835

After Mexico won her freedom from Spain in 1822, her territory stretched from the Yucatan peninsula north to the Oregon border. This is what Mexico looked like when Stephen Austin started his colony in 1823. Texas was in the province of Coahuila Y Texas whose capital was Saltillo.

WHEN MEXICO GAINED INDEPENDENCE FROM SPAIN IN 1821 SHE DEVISED AN ORDERLY SYSTEM BY WHICH AMERICANS COULD COLONIZE TEXAS. THE MEXICAN GOVERNMENT SET ASIDE VAST AREAS OR GRANTS AND APPOINTED LAND AGENTS TO SELL LAND WITHIN THESE GRANTS TO SETTLERS. THESE EARLY REAL ESTATE AGENTS WERE KNOWN AS

EMPRESARIOS.

EMPRESARIOS AGREED TO IMPORT 100 TO 800 FAMILIES WITHIN SIX YEARS. THEY WERE PROMISED A BONUS OF 2300 ACRES FOR EVERY 100 FAMILIES THEY BROUGHT IN AND WERE ALLOWED TO CHARGE EACH FAMILY A FEE OF $60 FOR SELLING THEM THEIR 4,428 ACRE "LOT."

AS THE OWNER OF A LEAD MINE AND SMELTER, 31 YEAR-OLD **MOSES AUSTIN** BECAME A PROSPEROUS BUSINESSMAN IN SOUTHWESTERN VIRGINIA BY 1792.

THE AUSTIN FAMILY

MOSES AND MARIA HAD TWO CHILDREN: STEPHEN, BORN NOVEMBER 3, 1793, AND EMILY, BORN TWO YEARS LATER.

BY 1796 AUSTIN'S LEAD MINES WERE PLAYING OUT AND HE BEGAN TO LOOK WESTWARD.

Missouri-Bound

MOSES AUSTIN HEARD ABOUT RICH DEPOSITS OF **LEAD** IN THE SPANISH COLONY OF MISSOURI. HE TRAVELED TO WASHINGTON, D.C. AND CONVINCED THE SPANISH MINISTER TO GIVE HIM WRITTEN PERMISSION TO INVESTIGATE.

LATE IN 1795 MOSES, THEN 35 YEARS OLD, LEFT VIRGINIA WITH HIS FAMILY AND A PARTY OF SLAVES AND MINERS AND HEADED WEST.

JUST OUTSIDE ST. LOUIS AUSTIN HALTED HIS GROUP AND HAD EVERYONE CHANGE INTO THEIR FINEST CLOTHING.

THEN THEY MADE A GRAND ENTRANCE INTO THE CITY.

AUSTIN'S COMPANY TOWN

IN 1796 THE SPANISH GOVERNOR OF MISSOURI GAVE MOSES AUSTIN A LARGE PARCEL OF LAND ON WHICH HE ESTABLISHED **POTOSI**, A TOWN STRUCTURED ON THE MINING AND SMELTING OF LEAD.

AUSTIN ERECTED FURNACES, A SHOT TOWER, A GENERAL STORE, AND HOUSING FOR SEVERAL HUNDRED MINERS, SLAVES, AND THEIR FAMILIES.

ST. LOUIS

POTOSI

MR. AUSTIN BECAME ONE OF THE MOST INFLUENTIAL MEN IN MISSOURI. HIS COLONY FLOURISHED FOR 20 YEARS.

YOUNG STEPHEN AUSTIN

MOSES AND MARIA AUSTIN HAD TWO CHILDREN WHO WERE BORN IN VIRGINIA, STEPHEN AND EMILY. THEIR SECOND SON, JAMES E. BROWN AUSTIN, WAS BORN IN MISSOURI IN 1803.

IN 1804 CONNECTICUT-BORN MOSES MADE A DECISION...

STEPHEN WE ARE SENDING YOU TO SCHOOL IN NEW ENGLAND.

A YANKEE VISITOR IN AUSTIN'S COLONY WAS RETURNING HOME. MOSES ENLISTED HIM TO PROVIDE A SAFE ESCORT FOR YOUNG STEPHEN TO FRIENDS IN CONNECTICUT. MR. AUSTIN ALSO SENT A LETTER INSTRUCTING HIS FRIENDS TO ENROLL HIS SON IN A GOOD SCHOOL.

Fatherly Advice

IT TOOK A FEW WEEKS FOR YOUNG STEPHEN AUSTIN TO TRAVEL BY KEELBOAT, THEN SAILING SHIP, TO COLCHESTER, CONNECTICUT.

THERE, IN 1804 HE WAS ENROLLED IN **BACON ACADEMY.**

THE SCHOOL PRINCIPAL RECEIVED A LETTER FROM MOSES AUSTIN

TO STEPHEN HE SENT ADVICE WHICH SAID, IN EFFECT...

"...STEPHEN SHOULD STUDY THE CLASSICKS... WRITE WELL... AND (DEVELOP) CORRECT MORAL PRINCIPLES OF THE FIRST CONSEQUENCE."

BE SOCIABLE... PAY YOUR OWN WAY... DO NOT BE A CHEAPSKATE... NEVER LOAN MONEY TO YOUR SCHOOL MATES.

STEPHEN REMAINED AT BACON ACADEMY FOR THREE YEARS.

College, Business, & Politics

AFTER LEAVING BACON ACADEMY IN CONNECTICUT, 13 YEAR-OLD STEPHEN AUSTIN CROSSED THE APPALACHIANS AND ENTERED TRANSYLVANIA UNIVERSITY IN LEXINGTON, KENTUCKY.

AUSTIN STUDIED LIBERAL ARTS AND GRADUATED IN 1810.

HE RETURNED TO MISSOURI AND, FOR THE NEXT TWO YEARS, MANAGED HIS FATHER'S STORE AND MINE AT BRETON.

IN 1814 STEPHEN WAS ELECTED TO THE TERRITORIAL LEGISLATURE OF MISSOURI.

LEAD and *Marriage*

MOSES AUSTIN ENTRUSTED THE MANAGEMENT OF HIS LEAD MINES NEAR POTOSI, MISSOURI TO HIS 19 YEAR-OLD SON, STEPHEN, IN 1812. UNFORTUNATELY THE COUNTRY WENT INTO AN ECONOMIC SLUMP AND AUSTIN'S LEAD BUSINESS BEGAN TO LOSE MONEY.

MEANWHILE, IN AUGUST 1813, STEPHEN'S SISTER, EMILY, MARRIED JAMES BRYAN. THEY SETTLED IN POTOSI AND HAD THREE SONS AND A DAUGHTER. THESE CHILDREN CARRIED ON THE AUSTIN LEGACY.

STEPHEN AUSTIN, THE FATHER OF TEXAS, NEVER MARRIED OR HAD ANY CHILDREN.

FINANCIAL RUIN

STEPHEN AUSTIN WAS MANAGING HIS FATHER'S LEAD MINES IN MISSOURI IN 1816.

MEANWHILE, MOSES AUSTIN HELPED START THE BANK OF ST. LOUIS AND WAS A PRINCIPAL STOCKHOLDER. THE BANK LOANED MONEY TO LAND SPECULATORS.

AN ECONOMIC DEPRESSION HIT THE COUNTRY IN 1819. SPECULATORS DEFAULTED ON THEIR LOANS. MANY BANKS COLLAPSED INCLUDING AUSTIN'S. CONSEQUENTLY, MOSES AUSTIN LOST EVERYTHING.

STEPHEN AUSTIN WENT LOOKING FOR A JOB IN NEW ORLEANS.

MOSES AUSTIN WAS 54 YEARS OLD AND BROKE. UNDAUNTED, HE SET HIS SIGHTS ON A NEW VENTURE IN TEXAS.

THE STRAIN FROM HIS TRIP TO TEXAS RESULTED IN THE

RUINED HEALTH

OF MOSES AUSTIN. IN JANUARY 1821 HE RETURNED HOME TO MISSOURI FROM HIS MEETING WITH GOVERNOR MARTINEZ IN SAN ANTONIO, TEXAS. HE WAS WEAK AND EXHAUSTED.

NEVERTHELESS HE CONTINUED TO MAKE ARRANGEMENTS FOR HIS COLONY.

"TO MY SON, STEPHEN, IN NEW ORLEANS: CHARTER A SHIP TO BRING SUPPLIES AND COLONISTS TO TEXAS."

FINALLY, IN MID MAY, AFTER WAITING FOUR MONTHS, MOSES RECEIVED WRITTEN APPROVAL FOR HIS COLONY FROM THE PROVINCIAL COUNCIL IN MEXICO.

MOSES RODE TO HAZEL RUN TO TELL HIS DAUGHTER THE GOOD NEWS. WHEN HE ARRIVED THERE HE COLLAPSED, SUFFERING FROM PNEUMONIA.

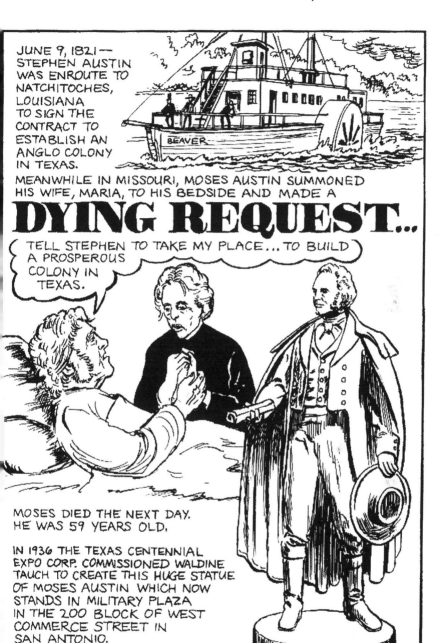

JUNE 9, 1821—STEPHEN AUSTIN WAS ENROUTE TO NATCHITOCHES, LOUISIANA TO SIGN THE CONTRACT TO ESTABLISH AN ANGLO COLONY IN TEXAS.

BEAVER

MEANWHILE IN MISSOURI, MOSES AUSTIN SUMMONED HIS WIFE, MARIA, TO HIS BEDSIDE AND MADE A

DYING REQUEST...

TELL STEPHEN TO TAKE MY PLACE... TO BUILD A PROSPEROUS COLONY IN TEXAS.

MOSES DIED THE NEXT DAY. HE WAS 59 YEARS OLD.

IN 1936 THE TEXAS CENTENNIAL EXPO CORP. COMMISSIONED WALDINE TAUCH TO CREATE THIS HUGE STATUE OF MOSES AUSTIN WHICH NOW STANDS IN MILITARY PLAZA IN THE 200 BLOCK OF WEST COMMERCE STREET IN SAN ANTONIO.

The Spanish Escort

STEPHEN AUSTIN AND HIS PARTY*ARRIVED AT NATCHITOCHES, LOUISIANA ON JUNE 26, 1821. HE WAS GREETED BY DON ERASMO SEGUIN AND J.M. BERRAMENDI, THE SPANISH AGENTS WHO GAVE HIM THE PERMIT FOR HIS FATHER'S COLONY.

ON JULY 3rd, SEGUIN AND BERRAMENDI BEGAN TO ESCORT MR. AUSTIN AND HIS MEN TO A MEETING WITH GOV. MARTINEZ IN SAN ANTONIO.

WHILE CAMPED ALONG THE SABINE RIVER ON JULY 10, A MESSAGE FOR STEPHEN ARRIVED, "...YOUR FATHER DIED ON JUNE 10..."

HE IMMEDIATELY WROTE HIS MOTHER, "... I SHALL CONTINUE FATHER'S UNDERTAKING."

* AUSTIN BROUGHT WITH HIM "8 TO 10 MEN" WHO WOULD EXPLORE THE COLONY.

STEPHEN TAKES OVER

IT TOOK SIX WEEKS FOR STEPHEN AUSTIN, HIS "EXPLORERS," AND THEIR SPANISH ESCORT TO TRAVEL FROM LOUISIANA TO SAN ANTONIO. THE TRIP WAS INTERRUPTED BY ILLNESS, HUNTING FORAYS, AND SEARCHING FOR A LOST TEAM MEMBER.

REACHING SAN ANTONIO ON AUG. 12, 1821, AUSTIN PROMPTLY MET WITH GOVERNOR MARTINEZ.

I HEREBY RECOGNIZE YOU AS THE HEIR TO YOUR FATHER'S COLONY.

YOU MAY NOW START TO EXPLORE THE LAND AND BRING IN SUPPLIES DUTY FREE.

Austin's Exploration

STEPHEN AUSTIN AND HIS MAPPING TEAM STARTED TO EXPLORE HIS COLONY ON AUGUST 21, 1821.

SAN ANTONIO

ALTHOUGH THE PERMIT FOR HIS COLONY ONLY AUTHORIZED HIM TO EXPLORE THE COLORADO RIVER, AUSTIN ALSO MAPPED PARTS OF THE SAN ANTONIO, GUADALUPE, AND BRAZOS RIVERS, PLUS A SECTION OF THE GULF COAST.

AUSTIN RETURNED TO LOUISIANA ON OCTOBER 1st. DURING THE PREVIOUS FIVE WEEKS HE TRAVERSED THE REGION THAT IS NOW COVERED BY TWENTY-THREE COUNTIES.

JUAN ERASMO SEGUIN

WAS BORN IN SAN ANTONIO IN 1782. HIS PUBLIC CAREER BEGAN IN 1807 WHEN HE WAS APPOINTED POSTMASTER OF SAN ANTONIO, A JOB HE HELD, ON AND OFF, UNTIL 1835.

IN 1821 JUAN ERASMO WAS ELECTED **ALCALDE**✱ OF SAN ANTONIO. ✱ A COMBINATION MAYOR, JUDGE, AND PRESIDENT OF THE CITY COUNCIL.

AT THE SAME TIME, SEGUIN'S PROMINENCE EARNED HIM THE ASSIGNMENT TO GIVE STEPHEN AUSTIN THE CONTRACT FOR HIS TEXAS COLONY AND ESCORT HIM TO SAN ANTONIO.

JONESBOROUGH

WAS ONE OF THE FIRST ANGLO-AMERICAN COMMUNITIES IN TEXAS. IT WAS NAMED AFTER HENRY JONES WHO, IN 1815, STARTED A FERRY SERVICE ACROSS THE RED RIVER.

IN 1821 THE U.S. GOVERNMENT EXPELLED WHITE SQUATTERS FROM THE OKLAHOMA INDIAN TERRITORY. MANY RESETTLED IN JONESBOROUGH.

A YEAR LATER SEVERAL JONESBOROUGH FAMILIES MOVED SOUTH TO JOIN STEPHEN AUSTIN'S COLONY.

Red River Port

BY 1830 JONESBOROUGH, TEXAS HAD BECOME A PROSPEROUS PORT ON THE RED RIVER. MERCHANTS WHO BASED THEIR COMPANIES HERE INCLUDED GEORGE W. WRIGHT, JAMES F. JOHNSTON, THAD W. RIKER, AND WILLIAM M. HARRISON.

THE TEXAS CONGRESS CHARTERED THE TOWN IN 1837. FIVE YEARS LATER A FLOOD DAMAGED MOST OF THE BUILDINGS AND SHIFTED THE RIVER CHANNEL A MILE TO THE NORTH, LEAVING JONESBOROUGH LANDLOCKED.

SOON THE TOWN WITHERED AWAY COMPLETELY. TODAY NOTHING REMAINS OF JONESBOROUGH.

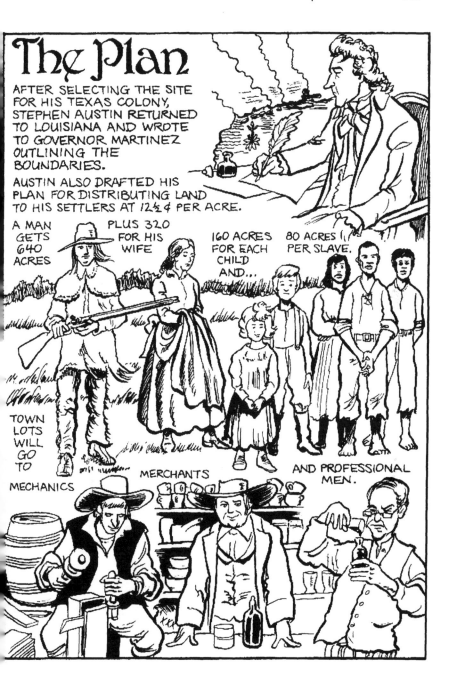

The Plan

AFTER SELECTING THE SITE FOR HIS TEXAS COLONY, STEPHEN AUSTIN RETURNED TO LOUISIANA AND WROTE TO GOVERNOR MARTINEZ OUTLINING THE BOUNDARIES.

AUSTIN ALSO DRAFTED HIS PLAN FOR DISTRIBUTING LAND TO HIS SETTLERS AT 12½¢ PER ACRE.

A MAN GETS 640 ACRES

PLUS 320 FOR HIS WIFE

160 ACRES FOR EACH CHILD AND...

80 ACRES PER SLAVE.

TOWN LOTS WILL GO TO MECHANICS

MERCHANTS

AND PROFESSIONAL MEN.

EARLY IN 1821 STEPHEN AUSTIN RESERVED TWO BOATS TO TAKE SETTLERS TO TEXAS. IN NOVEMBER HE BOUGHT ONE, THE

LIVELY.

AUSTIN'S PARTNER, JOE HAWKINS, FITTED IT WITH ENOUGH SUPPLIES FOR 300 SETTLERS.

AUSTIN RECRUITED ABOUT 17 MEN.

HE INSTRUCTED THEM TO SAIL TO THE MOUTH OF THE COLORADO RIVER, BUILD A FORT AND PLANT CROPS. AFTER A YEAR EACH MAN WOULD GET 640 ACRES AND PART OF THE HARVEST.

THE LIVELY LEFT NEW ORLEANS FOR TEXAS AND SOON VEERED OFF COURSE.

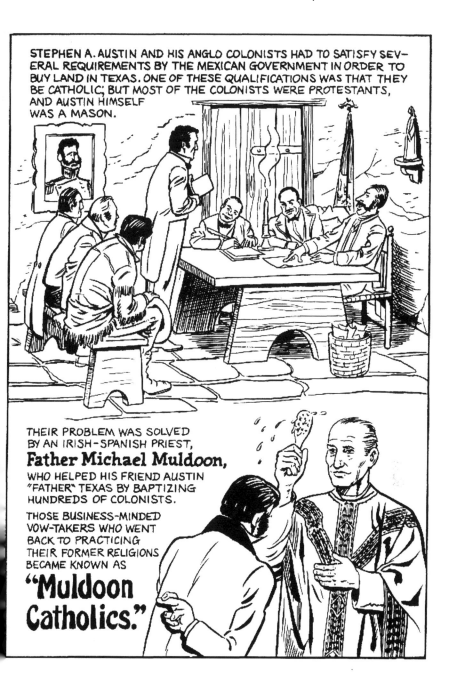

STEPHEN A. AUSTIN AND HIS ANGLO COLONISTS HAD TO SATISFY SEVERAL REQUIREMENTS BY THE MEXICAN GOVERNMENT IN ORDER TO BUY LAND IN TEXAS. ONE OF THESE QUALIFICATIONS WAS THAT THEY BE CATHOLIC; BUT MOST OF THE COLONISTS WERE PROTESTANTS, AND AUSTIN HIMSELF WAS A MASON.

THEIR PROBLEM WAS SOLVED BY AN IRISH-SPANISH PRIEST, **Father Michael Muldoon,** WHO HELPED HIS FRIEND AUSTIN "FATHER" TEXAS BY BAPTIZING HUNDREDS OF COLONISTS.

THOSE BUSINESS-MINDED VOW-TAKERS WHO WENT BACK TO PRACTICING THEIR FORMER RELIGIONS BECAME KNOWN AS

"Muldoon Catholics."

STEPHEN AUSTIN PLANNED TO MOVE MOST OF HIS "300" SETTLERS TO HIS TEXAS COLONY IN THE MIDDLE OF DECEMBER 1821.

HOWEVER, SOME WENT EARLIER. THESE WERE FARMERS WHO MOVED AFTER HARVESTING CROPS AT THEIR OLD PLACE AND WANTED TO START TO CLEAR THE LAND IN TEXAS AND PLANT NEW CROPS.

THE FIRST COLONIST

TO REACH THE COLONY WAS **ANDREW ROBINSON** WHO ARRIVED IN NOVEMBER 1821 WITH HIS WIFE, NANCY, AND THEIR TWO CHILDREN.

HE WAS SOON JOINED BY THREE BROTHERS & THEIR FAMILIES: ABNER, JOSEPH, AND ROBERT KUYKENDALL OF ARKANSAS.

ANDREW ROBINSON

WAS THE FIRST OF STEPHEN AUSTIN'S "OLD 300" COLONISTS TO SETTLE IN TEXAS. IN 1824 ROBINSON RECEIVED A GRANT OF 9,000 ACRES WHICH COVERED PRESENT-DAY BRAZORIA, WASHINGTON, AND WALLER COUNTIES.

APPOINTED CAPTAIN IN THE COLONIAL MILITIA, ROBINSON'S COMPANY FOUGHT THE KARANKAWAS IN SEPTEMBER 1824.

BY 1830 ROBINSON WAS OPERATING A FERRY AT LA BAHIA CROSSING ON THE BRAZOS RIVER.

ANDREW ALSO OWNED A HOTEL AND SALOON IN WASHINGTON, TEXAS, A TOWN HE HELPED FOUND ON HIS LAND GRANT IN 1833.

MR. ROBINSON DIED IN 1852.

Waiting for the *Lively*

OVER 200 FAMILIES MOVED TO AUSTIN'S COLONY IN TEXAS IN JANUARY AND FEBRUARY 1822. EACH FARMING FAMILY RECEIVED ONE *LABOR* (ALMOST 177 ACRES) AND EACH RANCHING FAMILY GOT ONE *SITIO* (ABOUT 4,428 ACRES).

MEANWHILE
STEPHEN AUSTIN WENT LOOKING FOR THE COLONISTS WHO WERE COMING TO TEXAS ON THE SLOOP *LIVELY*. THE VESSEL WAS SUPPOSED TO LAND AT THE MOUTH OF THE COLORADO RIVER.

THE *LIVELY* NEVER ARRIVED AT THE COLORADO RIVER.

SINCE THE BOAT CARRIED MOST OF THE COLONY'S PROVISIONS, THE SETTLERS HAD TO LIVE WITHOUT BREAD AND VEGETABLES FOR ABOUT SIX MONTHS.

THE SLOOP *LIVELY* WAS BOUND FOR TEXAS WITH TWENTY COLONISTS AND MOST OF THE PROVISIONS FOR AUSTIN'S COLONY.

The Lost Colonists

THEY HAD PLANNED TO RENDEVOUS WITH STEPHEN AUSTIN AT THE MOUTH OF THE COLORADO RIVER. NOT KNOWING THE DIFFERENCE, THE SKIPPER DROPPED ANCHOR 38 MILES SHORT—AT THE BRAZOS.

THE *LIVELY* RETURNED TO NEW ORLEANS. THE LOST COLONISTS TREKKED INLAND TO HIGHER GROUND, THEN SPENT THE NEXT FEW MONTHS IN A FRUITLESS SEARCH FOR THE MAIN BODY OF AUSTIN'S COLONY.

DISCOURAGED, THE LOST COLONISTS GAVE UP AND WENT BACK TO THE UNITED STATES.

COMANCHE HOLD-UP

STEPHEN AUSTIN, HIS INTERPRETER-DR. ROBERT ANDREWS, AND A MAN CALLED MR. WATERS, LEFT SAN ANTONIO FOR MEXICO CITY IN MARCH 1822.

A REVOLUTION HAD CONVERTED TEXAS FROM A SPANISH COLONY TO A MEXICAN PROVINCE. THEREFORE AUSTIN HAD TO CALL ON THE NEW GOVERNMENT AND REAPPLY FOR HIS LAND GRANT.

AFTER TRAVELING ABOUT 100 MILES THEY ENCOUNTERED SOME 50 COMANCHES WHO DEMANDED ALL OF THEIR BELONGINGS.

Time Well Spent

BY MARCH 1823 STEPHEN AUSTIN HAD BEEN IN MEXICO CITY ELEVEN MONTHS AWAITING THE APPROVAL OF HIS TEXAS COLONY. HIS WELL-BRED MANNER, HIS CONCERN FOR LOCAL PROBLEMS, AND THE PAINS HE TOOK TO LEARN FLUENT SPANISH ENDEARED HIM TO THE MEXICAN PEOPLE.

WOULD-BE *EMPRESARIOS*, AMERICANS SEEKING LAND GRANTS IN TEXAS, CAME TO SEÑOR AUSTIN FOR ADVICE.

AS A RESULT OF HIS TIME IN MEXICO, AUSTIN WAS THE ONLY MAN WITH THE SAVVY AND DIPLOMATIC SKILLS TO GUIDE TEXAS THROUGH MEXICAN POLITICS FOR THE NEXT DECADE.

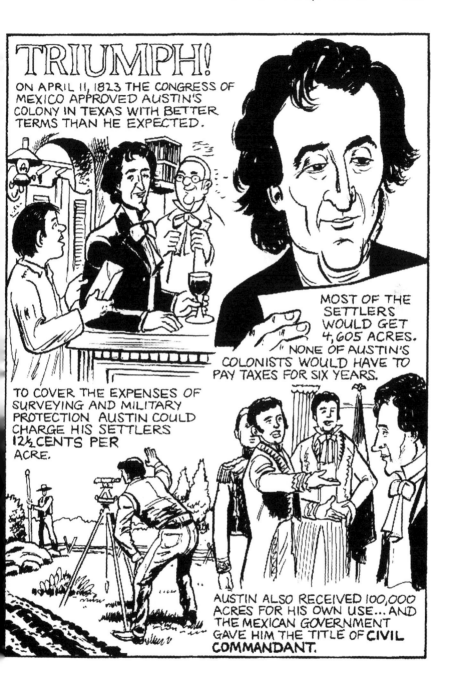

TRIUMPH!

ON APRIL 11, 1823 THE CONGRESS OF MEXICO APPROVED AUSTIN'S COLONY IN TEXAS WITH BETTER TERMS THAN HE EXPECTED.

MOST OF THE SETTLERS WOULD GET 4,605 ACRES. NONE OF AUSTIN'S COLONISTS WOULD HAVE TO PAY TAXES FOR SIX YEARS.

TO COVER THE EXPENSES OF SURVEYING AND MILITARY PROTECTION AUSTIN COULD CHARGE HIS SETTLERS 12½ CENTS PER ACRE.

AUSTIN ALSO RECEIVED 100,000 ACRES FOR HIS OWN USE... AND THE MEXICAN GOVERNMENT GAVE HIM THE TITLE OF **CIVIL COMMANDANT.**

WITH STEPHEN AUSTIN BACK IN TEXAS HIS COLONY STARTED TO IMPROVE. MANY PEOPLE WHO HAD GONE BACK EAST DECIDED TO RETURN. NEWCOMERS ALSO ARRIVED.

BY LATE 1824 BARON de BASTROP, AUSTIN'S LAND COMMISSIONER, HAD ISSUED 297 TITLES. AUSTIN FELL THREE FAMILIES SHORT OF THE 300 FAMILIES HE HAD CONTRACTED TO BRING TO TEXAS. AT ANY RATE, THE 297 BECAME KNOWN AS

THE OLD 300.

The First Texan of Wealth

BECAUSE OF THE VAST AMOUNT OF MONEY, LIVESTOCK, AND SLAVES HE BROUGHT INTO TEXAS, THE MEXICAN GOVERNMENT GRANTED TEN LEAGUES OF LAND TO JARED ELLISON GROCE ON JULY 29, 1824. HIS HOLDINGS SPREAD OVER PRESENT-DAY GRIMES AND WALLER COUNTIES.

SOON GROCE HAD A MANSION ATOP A HILL ON HIS BERNARDO PLANTATION NEAR HEMPSTEAD, WALLER COUNTY, WHERE HE LIVED UNTIL THE MALARIA EPIDEMIC OF 1833.

MR. GROCE IS SHOWN HERE WITH ONE OF HIS DAUGHTERS.

JARED GROCE, THE WEALTHIEST MAN IN AUSTIN'S COLONY, CULTIVATED WHAT WAS PROBABLY THE FIRST COTTON CROP IN TEXAS. OVER 90 SLAVES HARVESTED THE CROP IN 1822 ON HIS BERNARDO PLANTATION IN PRESENT-DAY GRIMES AND WALLER COUNTIES.

WHEN GROCE'S SON LEONARD FINISHED COLLEGE IN GEORGIA IN 1825 HE BROUGHT HOME TO TEXAS WHAT IS BELIEVED TO BE

THE FIRST COTTON GIN IN TEXAS.

IN OCTOBER 1823 STEPHEN AUSTIN, ACCOMPANIED BY BARON de BASTROP, CHOSE THE SITE FOR THE UNOFFICIAL CAPITAL OF HIS COLONY—A HIGH, EASILY DEFENSIBLE BLUFF FIFTEEN MILES FROM THE MALARIAL SWAMPS OF THE GULF COAST AND 175 MILES EAST OF SAN ANTONIO.

AUSTIN ALSO LIKED ITS CENTRAL LOCATION AND SOURCES OF FRESH WATER.

FELIPE de la GARZA, THE GOVERNOR OF THE EASTERN INTERIOR PROVINCES OF MEXICO GAVE THE TOWN ITS NAME.

IT WILL HONOR MY PATRON SAINT AND THE EMPRESARIO,

SAN FELIPE DE AUSTIN.

FELIPE ~ST. PHILIP OF BETHSAIDA WAS ONE OF THE TWELVE APOSTLES OF JESUS. PHILIP IS GREEK FOR LOVER OF HORSES.

AUSTIN'S CAPITAL

AROUND NOVEMBER 1823 SETH INGRAM BEGAN SURVEYING A FIVE LEAGUE EXPANSE OF PRAIRIE AND WOODLAND WHICH WOULD ENCOMPASS THE TOWN OF SAN FELIPE de AUSTIN.

THE TOWN'S DESIGN FOLLOWED THE MEXICAN STYLE—A REGULAR GRID OF STREETS AND AVENUES DOMINATED BY FOUR LARGE PLAZAS. BY 1828 SAN FELIPE HAD THREE GENERAL STORES, TWO TAVERNS, A HOTEL, BLACKSMITH SHOP, AND ABOUT 50 HOUSES FOR 200 CITIZENS.

GENERAL STORE

THE FIRST RANGERS

AS EMPRESARIO STEPHEN AUSTIN WAS COMMISSIONED A **LT. COLONEL** IN THE MEXICAN ARMY. HE WAS BOTH THE MILITARY AND POLITICAL BOSS OF HIS COLONY.

TO FIGHT OFF INDIAN RAIDS HE HIRED TEN MEN IN 1823 AND PAID THEM OUT OF HIS OWN POCKET.

ALTHOUGH AUSTIN CALLED THEM RANGERS, THE GROUP WAS ACTUALLY A LOCAL MILITIA.

HARDLY ANY RECORDS EXIST OF AUSTIN'S RANGERS.

STEPHEN AUSTIN'S GOVERNMENT,

AND THOSE OF OTHER EMPRESARIOS, FOLLOWED THE HISPANIC SYSTEM. THE MAJOR UNIT OF LOCAL GOVERNMENT WAS THE MUNICIPALITY CONSISTING OF SEVERAL TOWNS AND THOUSANDS OF SQUARE MILES. AUSTIN'S COLONY WAS A **MUNICIPALITY.**

THE *AYUNTAMIENTO* WAS THE GOVERNING COUNCIL OF THE MUNICIPALITY. ITS MEMBERS WERE CALLED *REGIDORES.* THE CHIEF EXECUTIVE OFFICER OF THE *AYUNTAMIENTO* WAS THE *ALCALDE,* A COMBINATION MAYOR, JUDGE, AND HIGH SHERIFF.

THE *AYUNTAMIENTO* OF AUSTIN'S COLONY FIRST MET IN MARCH 1828.

THE FIRST *ALCALDE* OF AUSTIN'S COLONY WAS TOM DUKE.

—REGIDORES—
HUMPHREY HOSEA LEAGUE
JACKSON

JOHN HOLTHAM, SECRETARY

LAURENCE R. KENNY, A LAWYER, WAS THE *SÍNDICO*—THE COLONY'S NOTARY-ATTORNEY-CONSTABLE.

PUBLIC EDUCATION

IN OLD SPANISH TEXAS WAS VIRTUALLY NON-EXISTENT. AROUND 1812 A PUBLIC SCHOOL WAS ESTABLISHED IN SAN ANTONIO BUT IT DID NOT LAST. A PRIVATE SOLDIER, JOSE GALAN, TAUGHT SCHOOL IN LA BAHIA IN 1818.

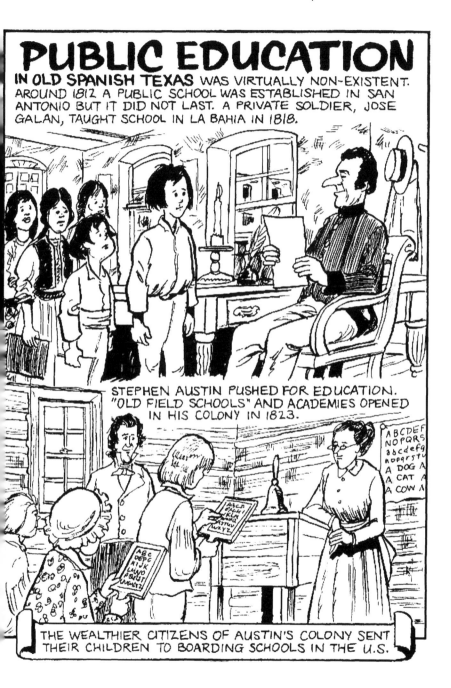

STEPHEN AUSTIN PUSHED FOR EDUCATION. "OLD FIELD SCHOOLS" AND ACADEMIES OPENED IN HIS COLONY IN 1823.

THE WEALTHIER CITIZENS OF AUSTIN'S COLONY SENT THEIR CHILDREN TO BOARDING SCHOOLS IN THE U.S.

The Bachelor Father of Texas

STEPHEN AUSTIN NEVER MARRIED. HE DEVOTED HIS LIFE TO TEXAS. PROSPECTIVE COLONISTS STAYED AT HIS HOUSE. HE PERMITTED ELECTIONS FOR REGIDORES AND ALCALDES TO RUN HIS COLONY, AND HE ACTED AS AGENT FOR PLANTERS WHO WANTED TO DO BUSINESS WITH FIRMS IN THE U.S.

SOUTHERN PARENTS CONSTANTLY WROTE HIM TO KEEP A LOOK-OUT FOR THEIR OFF-SPRING WHO MAY HAVE RUN AWAY TO TEXAS.

AFTER HIS FIRST 300 PATENTS WERE TAKEN, AUSTIN REQUESTED AND GOT MORE. BY 1835 HE HAD ATTRACTED 1,500 AMERICAN FAMILIES WHO BECAME THE FOUNDATION OF ANGLO-TEXAS.

THE RUSH TO COLONIZE

STEPHEN AUSTIN RECEIVED HIS EMPRESARIO GRANT UNDER MEXICO'S IMPERIAL COLONIZATION LAW OF 1823.

A SHORT TIME LATER EMPEROR ITURBIDE WAS OVERTHROWN,

THE 1823 LAW WAS REPEALED BUT AUSTIN WAS PERMITTED TO KEEP HIS CONTRACT TO COLONIZE TEXAS.

THE NEW GOVERNMENT APPROVED A NATIONAL COLONIZATION LAW IN 1824 WHICH ALLOWED THEIR PROVINCES TO DOLE OUT CONTRACTS TO COLONIZERS. TEXAS WAS IN THE PROVINCE OF COAHUILA Y TEXAS.

THE STATE OF COAHUILA Y TEXAS PASSED ITS COLONIZATION LAW ON MARCH 24, 1825. IMMEDIATELY PROSPECTIVE EMPRESARIOS LINED UP FOR LAND GRANTS IN TEXAS.

The Empresario Grants

FROM 1824 TO 1835, TWENTY-SEVEN DIFFERENT PARTIES SIGNED FORTY-ONE EMPRESARIO CONTRACTS WITH THE GOVERNMENT OF MEXICO. THE RESULT WAS A PATCHWORK OF COLONIES THAT STRETCHED FROM LOUISIANA TO THE NUECES RIVER.

DR. JAMES HEWETSON

JAMES POWER

LORENZO de ZAVALA

THE BOUNDARIES OF THE MAJOR EMPRESARIO GRANTS ARE SUPERIMPOSED OVER A CONTEMPORARY MAP OF TEXAS COUNTIES.

Cameron

Cameron | Austin & Williams (Later Robertson's Colony) | Filisola

Burnet | Nacogdoches

Zavala

Woodbury | Austin | Vehlein

San Felipe

San Antonio | Gonzales | Austin's Colony

DeWitt | La Bahia | Galveston Island

McMullen & McGloin | Victoria | De Leon

Refugio

Power & Hewetson

NOT EVERY EMPRESARIO SUCCEEDED IN BRINGING 100 TO 800 FAMILIES TO TEXAS WITHIN SIX YEARS.

The Irish Empresarios

FOUR IRISHMEN RECEIVED LAND GRANTS FROM MEXICO AND FOUNDED TWO SETTLEMENTS IN TEXAS. JOHN McMULLEN AND JAMES McGLOIN WERE ABLE TO ROUND UP THREE BOATLOADS OF IRISH IMMIGRANTS TO SETTLE THE **SAN PATRICIO** COLONY BETWEEN 1829 AND 1833. THIS SITE WAS SCOUTED AND FIRST SETTLED IN 1826 BY JAMES O'REILLY AND JEREMIAH O'TOOLE AND THEIR FAMILIES.

THE OTHER IRISH COLONY, **REFUGIO**, WAS FOUNDED BY JAMES POWER AND JAMES HEWETSON IN 1834. NOT ALL OF THE PEOPLE IN THESE COLONIES WERE IRISH. THE EMPRESARIOS-McMULLEN, McGLOIN, POWER AND HEWETSON - WERE REQUIRED TO GUARANTEE THE RIGHTS AND PROPERTY OF THE MEXICANS ALREADY LIVING THERE. ALSO, OTHER NATIONALITIES MOVED TO THESE COLONIES.

NEXT TO STEPHEN AUSTIN THE MOST IMPORTANT EMPRESARIO IN TEXAS WAS ANOTHER MISSOURIAN NAMED

GREEN DEWITT.

HE TRIED TO OBTAIN AN EMPRESARIO GRANT IN 1822 BUT THE MEXICAN AUTHORITIES TURNED HIM DOWN.

THREE YEARS LATER HE WENT TO SALTILLO, CAPITAL OF THE COAHUILA Y TEXAS PROVINCE, AND REAPPLIED.

THIS TIME, WITH THE HELP OF AUSTIN AND BARON de BASTROP, HE RECEIVED A CONTRACT ON APRIL 15, 1825 TO SETTLE 400 COLONISTS NEAR AUSTIN'S COLONY.
CONTINUED...

DEWITT'S COLONY

WAS MADE POSSIBLE WHEN, IN 1825, SARA SEELY DEWITT SOLD HER PROPERTY IN MISSOURI AND GAVE THE PROFITS TO HER HUSBAND, GREEN.

THE DEWITTS MOVED TO TEXAS IN 1826 WITH THEIR TWO SONS AND THREE DAUGHTERS.

MR. DEWITT USED THE MONEY FROM THE SALE TO DEVELOP HIS COLONY. HELPING HIM WERE JAMES KERR, JOSE NAVARRO, AND BYRD & CHARLES LOCKHART.

SHOWN HERE IS DEWITT'S COLONY SUPERIMPOSED OVER PRESENT-DAY COUNTIES.

BASTROP
CALDWELL
FAYETTE
COLORADO
GUADALUPE
SEGUIN
GONZALES
HALLETTSVILLE
WILSON
GONZALES
LAVACA
KARNES
DEWITT
CUERO
JACKSON
VICTORIA
GOLIAD
VICTORIA

GREEN DEWITT APPOINTED **JAMES KERR** TO THE MOST IMPORTANT JOB IN HIS COLONY, SURVEYOR-GENERAL.

IN AUGUST 1825, KERR ALONG WITH ERASTUS "DEAF" SMITH, BRAZIL DURBIN, GERON HINDS, JOHN WIGHTMAN, JAMES MUSICK, AND A MR. STRICKLAND SELECTED A SITE FOR THE CAPITAL OF DEWITT'S COLONY.

THEY BUILT SOME CABINS AT THE JUNCTION OF THE GUADALUPE AND SAN MARCOS RIVERS AND NAMED IT

GONZALES IN HONOR

OF THE GOVERNOR OF THE PROVINCE OF COAHUILA Y TEXAS, DON RAFAEL GONZALES.

MARTIN DE LEON

WAS THE ONLY **MEXICAN EMPRESARIO** TO ORGANIZE A COLONY IN TEXAS. BORN IN 1765 TO RICH ARISTOCRATIC PARENTS IN TAMAULIPAS, MEXICO, HE PASSED UP A CHANCE TO STUDY IN EUROPE. INSTEAD HE SOLD MINING SUPPLIES.

HE MARRIED PATRICIA de la GARZA, DAUGHTER OF A GENERAL. THEY MOVED TO TEXAS IN 1805 AND ESTABLISHED A LARGE RANCH.

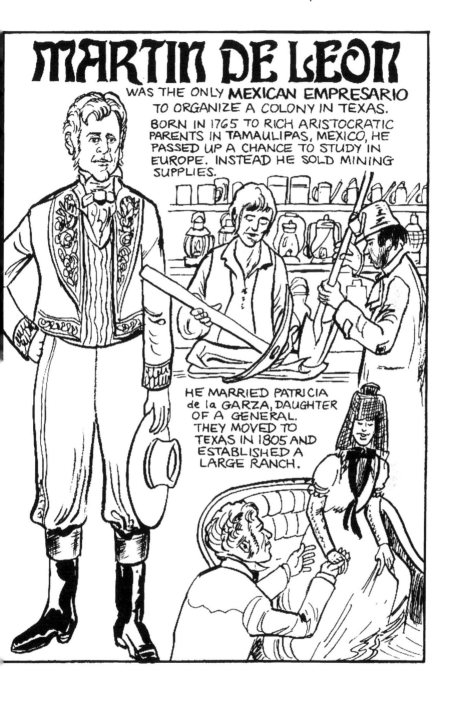

The Mexican Empresario

BEGINNING IN 1807, DON MARTIN DE LEON TRIED TO START A COLONY IN TEXAS BUT THE GOVERNMENT OF NEW SPAIN KEPT TURNING HIM DOWN.

THEN, IN 1824, AFTER MEXICO WON INDEPENDENCE FROM SPAIN, THE NEW GOVERNMENT APPROVED DE LEON'S PETITION TO SETTLE 41 MEXICAN FAMILIES IN WHAT ARE NOW CALHOUN AND VICTORIA COUNTIES, AND PART OF LAVACA, JACKSON, AND DEWITT COUNTIES.

DE LEON'S COLONY,

THE ONLY PREDOMINANTLY MEXICAN COLONY IN TEXAS, WAS ESTABLISHED IN 1824 BY MARTIN DE LEON. BY OCTOBER HE AND TWELVE FAMILIES HAD SETTLED ALONG THE GUADALUPE RIVER AT CYPRESS GROVE.

BETWEEN 1824 AND 1835 THE MEXICAN GOVERNMENT ISSUED LAND GRANTS TO DE LEON'S COLONISTS. EACH SETTLER RECEIVED ONE LEAGUE (3 MILES) OF GRAZING LAND, A TOWN LOT, AND ONE LABOR (177 ACRES) OF ARABLE LAND.

IN 1824 THE MEXICAN EMPRESARIO DON MARTIN DE LEON SELECTED A SITE FOR HIS CAPITAL AT CYPRESS GROVE AND NAMED IT GUADALUPE

VICTORIA.

DE LEON

DE LEON'S SON-IN-LAW JOSE M.J. CARBAJAL LAID OUT AND SURVEYED THE TOWN.

THE NAMESAKE OF VICTORIA WAS THE FIRST PRESIDENT OF MEXICO AND A CLOSE FRIEND OF DE LEON, GUADALUPE VICTORIA.

DEWITT'S ARREST

EMPRESARIO GREEN DEWITT WAS ARRESTED FOR SMUGGLING IN 1826 BUT STEPHEN AUSTIN INTERVENED AND DEWITT WAS RELEASED.

IN JULY 1827 DEWITT WENT TO THE UNITED STATES TO ENLIST MORE SETTLERS FOR HIS COLONY IN TEXAS.

IN HIS ABSENCE, POLITICAL CHIEF SAUCEDO ORDERED ALL OF DEWITT'S COLONISTS TO ABANDON THE PORT OF OLD STATION AND MOVE TO GONZALES.

AS A RESULT, IMMIGRANTS TO DEWITT'S COLONY WOULD HAVE TO TREK OVERLAND TO TEXAS, AN ARDUOUS AND DANGEROUS JOURNEY.

DEWITT COULD NOT RECRUIT ENOUGH COLONISTS, SO HIS EMPRESARIO CONTRACT WAS CANCELLED IN 1831. DELEON TOOK OVER HIS COLONY.

The Downfall of DeWitt's Colony

THE MEXICAN GOVERNMENT PASSED A LAW IN 1830 PROHIBITING ALL IMMIGRATION INTO TEXAS. DEWITT'S COLONY WAS STALLED AT 531 CITIZENS. THE ONLY TOWN, GONZALES, HAD ONLY 20 STRUCTURES AND NEVER BECAME A COMMERCIAL HUB.

THE COLONY WAS A FINANCIAL STRAIN ON GREEN DEWITT.

GONZALES

DEWITT ALSO FAILED TO BRING 400 FAMILIES TO TEXAS AS STIPULATED IN HIS EMPRESARIO CONTRACT.

THE MEXICANS REFUSED TO RENEW HIS CONTRACT. IN 1835 MR. DEWITT WENT TO MONCLOVA TO BUY LAND. HE DIED THERE OF CHOLERA.

Ernst's Place

JOHANN ERNST, A GERMAN IMMIGRANT, BUILT A HOUSE FOR HIS LARGE FAMILY ON THE EASTERN EDGE OF HIS LAND GRANT IN AUSTIN'S COLONY IN 1832. IT STOOD NEAR THE ROAD FROM SAN FELIPE TO BASTROP.

OVER THE YEARS THE HOUSE BECAME A HOTEL AND BOARDINGHOUSE FOR TRAVELERS AND IMMIGRANTS. MR. ERNST EVEN LOANED MONEY TO NEW SETTLERS, EARNING HIM THE SOBRIQUET *FATHER OF THE IMMIGRANTS*.

JOHANN ERNST STARTED TO DEVELOP HIS LAND IN AUSTIN'S COLONY (NOW AUSTIN COUNTY) IN 1833. HE GREW TOBACCO, ROLLED IT INTO CIGARS, AND SOLD THEM IN GALVESTON, HOUSTON...

AND SAN FELIPE.

ERNST'S CIGAR BUSINESS PROSPERED AND HE HIRED SO MANY WORKERS THAT HE LAID OUT A TOWN ON HIS PROPERTY. HIS ANGLO NEIGHBORS SAID THE GERMAN RESIDENTS WERE INDUSTRIOUS SO ERNST NAMED HIS TOWN *INDUSTRY*. IT WAS *THE FIRST PERMANENT GERMAN SETTLEMENT IN TEXAS.*

CIGAR

Another Empresario

CALLING THEMSELVES THE **TEXAS ASSOCIATION**, A CONSORTIUM OF 70 BUSINESSMEN AND FARMERS IN NASHVILLE, TENNESSEE SENT ROBERT LEFTWICH TO MEXICO CITY IN MARCH 1822 WITH A FORMAL REQUEST TO SETTLE 800 FAMILIES IN TEXAS.

LEFTWICH NEGOTIATED WITH THE MEXICAN GOVERNMENT FOR THREE YEARS. MEANWHILE THE MONEY THAT THE ASSOCIATION HAD ADVANCED HIM RAN OUT. WHEN THE REQUEST WAS FINALLY APPROVED...

LEFTWICH BORROWED MONEY TO PAY FOR THE EMPRESARIO CONTRACT. THEREFORE HE HAD THE DOCUMENT MADE OUT IN HIS OWN NAME.

The Austin & Williams Contract

AUSTIN

WILLIAMS

IN 1831 STEPHEN AUSTIN AND HIS SECRETARY, SAMUEL MAY WILLIAMS, TOOK OVER THE EMPRESARIO CONTRACT WHICH ORIGINALLY BELONGED TO THE NASHVILLE COMPANY.

STERLING CLACK ROBERTSON, SPOKESMAN FOR THE NASHVILLE COMPANY, DID NOT TAKE THIS LYING DOWN. HE FILED A SERIES OF LAWSUITS THAT DRAGGED ON FOR YEARS AND DELAYED THE SETTLING OF CENTRAL TEXAS.

FINALLY ON MAY 18, 1834 THE GOVERNMENT CANCELLED THE AUSTIN & WILLIAMS CONTRACT AND...

NAMED STERLING ROBERTSON AS THE EMPRESARIO.

AFTERWARDS CENTRAL TEXAS WAS KNOWN AS ROBERTSON'S COLONY.

ROBERTSON'S COLONY

IN 1834 THE LEGISLATURE OF COAHUILA RECOGNIZED STERLING CLACK ROBERTSON AS THE EMPRESARIO OF THE FORMER AUSTIN & WILLIAMS COLONY IN EAST-CENTRAL TEXAS.

ROBERTSON'S OBLIGATION WAS TO ENTICE 800 FAMILIES TO SETTLE IN HIS COLONY. EACH FAMILY WOULD RECEIVE 177 ACRES.

HE PLACED THE CAPITAL OF HIS DOMAIN NEAR PRESENT-DAY MARLIN, FALLS COUNTY.

HE NAMED IT SARAHVILLE de VIESCA...

AFTER HIS MOTHER, SARAH, WHO PUT UP MONEY FOR HIS COLONY AND...

AUGUSTIN VIESCA WHO PRESIDED OVER THE MEXICAN LEGISLATURE WHEN IT GRANTED THE CONTRACT.

SARAHVILLE WAS ABANDONED IN 1836 DURING THE TEXAS REVOLUTION.

THIS MAP SHOWS THE PRESENT-DAY COUNTIES THAT WERE
PART OF LEFTWICH'S GRANT (1825-1830), AUSTIN AND WILLIAMS'S
COLONY (1830-1834), AND FINALLY ROBERTSON'S COLONY.

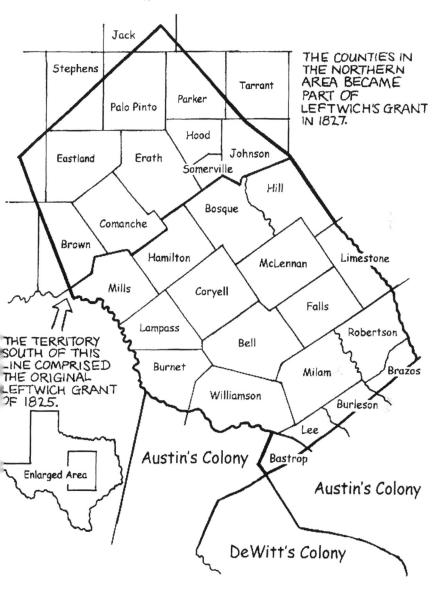

THE COUNTIES IN
THE NORTHERN
AREA BECAME
PART OF
LEFTWICH'S GRANT
IN 1827.

THE TERRITORY
SOUTH OF THIS
LINE COMPRISED
THE ORIGINAL
LEFTWICH GRANT
OF 1825.

Enlarged Area

Jack
Stephens
Palo Pinto
Parker
Tarrant
Hood
Eastland
Erath
Somerville
Johnson
Hill
Bosque
Comanche
Brown
Hamilton
McLennan
Limestone
Mills
Coryell
Falls
Lampass
Bell
Robertson
Burnet
Milam
Brazos
Williamson
Burleson
Lee
Austin's Colony
Bastrop
Austin's Colony
DeWitt's Colony

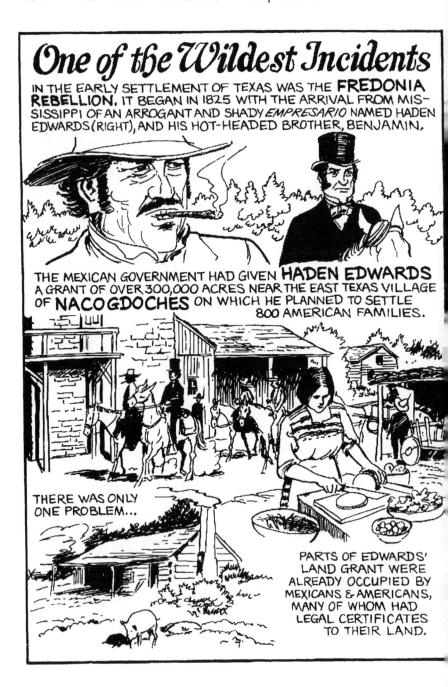

One of the Wildest Incidents

IN THE EARLY SETTLEMENT OF TEXAS WAS THE **FREDONIA REBELLION.** IT BEGAN IN 1825 WITH THE ARRIVAL FROM MISSISSIPPI OF AN ARROGANT AND SHADY *EMPRESARIO* NAMED HADEN EDWARDS (RIGHT), AND HIS HOT-HEADED BROTHER, BENJAMIN.

THE MEXICAN GOVERNMENT HAD GIVEN **HADEN EDWARDS** A GRANT OF OVER 300,000 ACRES NEAR THE EAST TEXAS VILLAGE OF **NACOGDOCHES** ON WHICH HE PLANNED TO SETTLE 800 AMERICAN FAMILIES.

THERE WAS ONLY ONE PROBLEM...

PARTS OF EDWARDS' LAND GRANT WERE ALREADY OCCUPIED BY MEXICANS & AMERICANS, MANY OF WHOM HAD LEGAL CERTIFICATES TO THEIR LAND.

Haden Edwards' Ultimatum

THE MEXICAN GOVERNMENT DESIGNATED HADEN EDWARDS AN *EMPRESARIO*, GRANTING HIM 300,000+ ACRES IN EAST TEXAS ON WHICH HE COULD DEVELOP A COLONY.

HADEN IMMEDIATELY POSTED A NOTICE IN NACOGDOCHES...

THIS BROUGHT THE *EARLIER* SETTLERS CLAMORING TO THE MEXICAN AUTHORITIES.

I OWN MY SPREAD FAIR 'N' SQUARE!

I DON'T HAVE TA SHOW ANYTHING TA EDWARDS!

JUST AS THINGS WERE COMING TO A BOIL, HADEN LEFT ON A BUSINESS TRIP TO THE UNITED STATES, LEAVING HIS TYRANNICAL BROTHER, BENJAMIN, IN CHARGE.

THE ANNULMENT OF HADEN EDWARDS' EMPRESARIO CONTRACT SENT HIS BROTHER, BEN, ON THE WARPATH. HE NEEDED ALLIES, SO HE MADE A TREATY WITH THE **CHEROKEES** WHO HAD MIGRATED INTO EAST TEXAS, BUT WERE DISGRUNTLED BECAUSE MEXICO REFUSED TO GIVE THEM ANY LAND.

HOWEVER, THE INDIANS WHO SIGNED THAT PACT HAD NO AUTHORITY, AND IT WAS DISAVOWED BY THE TRIBAL COUNCIL.

UNAWARE OF THIS, BEN EDWARDS AND 30 OF HIS COLONISTS RODE INTO NACOGDOCHES ON DECEMBER 16 1826, SEIZED THE FORT, DECLARED INDEPENDENCE FROM MEXICO, AND PROCLAIMED

the Republic of Fredonia.

The Fredonian Rebellion

LASTED ABOUT SIX WEEKS, FROM MID DEC. 1826 TO LATE JAN. 1827. AFTER PROCLAIMING THEMSELVES THE REPUBLIC OF FREDONIA, BEN EDWARDS AND 30 OF HIS COLONISTS HOLED UP IN THE FORT AT NACOGDOCHES AND FOUGHT THE LOCAL MILITIA.

EDWARDS ASKED STEPHEN AUSTIN FOR HELP. NOT ONLY DID AUSTIN REFUSE, BUT...

HE ASSIGNED 100 OF HIS AMERICAN COLONISTS TO COLONEL AHUMADA'S MEXICAN REGIMENT THAT WAS MARCHING ON THE REBELS. IN RETURN, AHUMADA PROMISED AMNESTY TO ANY FREDONIAN WHO SURRENDERED.

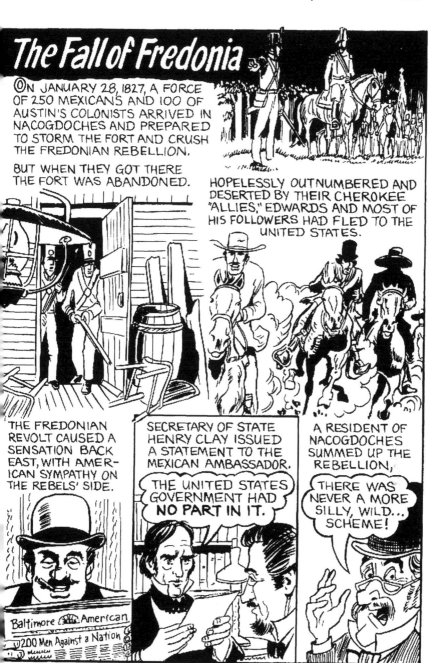

The Fall of Fredonia

ON JANUARY 28, 1827, A FORCE OF 250 MEXICANS AND 100 OF AUSTIN'S COLONISTS ARRIVED IN NACOGDOCHES AND PREPARED TO STORM THE FORT AND CRUSH THE FREDONIAN REBELLION.

BUT WHEN THEY GOT THERE THE FORT WAS ABANDONED.

HOPELESSLY OUTNUMBERED AND DESERTED BY THEIR CHEROKEE "ALLIES," EDWARDS AND MOST OF HIS FOLLOWERS HAD FLED TO THE UNITED STATES.

THE FREDONIAN REVOLT CAUSED A SENSATION BACK EAST, WITH AMERICAN SYMPATHY ON THE REBELS' SIDE.

Baltimore American
200 Men Against a Nation

SECRETARY OF STATE HENRY CLAY ISSUED A STATEMENT TO THE MEXICAN AMBASSADOR.

THE UNITED STATES GOVERNMENT HAD **NO PART IN IT.**

A RESIDENT OF NACOGDOCHES SUMMED UP THE REBELLION,

THERE WAS NEVER A MORE SILLY, WILD... SCHEME!

Part Four

People and Places

The location of places mentioned in this section are shown on this map.

BEFORE THE TEXAS REVOLUTION (1836) THE SHALLOW WATERS OF **CORPUS CHRISTI BAY** WERE PROTECTED BY OFFSHORE ISLANDS, MAKING IT AN EXCELLENT HAVEN FOR

SMUGGLERS

HENRY KINNEY FOUNDED THE CITY OF CORPUS CHRISTI IN 1839. THE REPUBLIC OF TEXAS ACCUSED HIM OF ILLEGALLY TRADING WITH MEXICO. NOTHING CAME OF THE ACCUSATION AND KINNEY BECAME A SENATOR.

DURING THE CIVIL WAR CORPUS CHRISTI REMAINED A MAJOR PORT FOR CONFEDERATE BLOCKADE RUNNERS UNTIL THE YANKEES CAPTURED THE HARBOR IN 1864.

Lincoln's Partner

GEORGE WASHINGTON **GLASSCOCK** WAS BORN IN 1811 IN KENTUCKY.

BY 1832 HE HAD MOVED TO SPRINGFIELD, ILLINOIS AND WAS IN PARTNERSHIP WITH ABRAHAM LINCOLN. THEY RAN FLATBOATS ON THE SANGAMON RIVER.

GLASSCOCK MOVED TO ZAVALLA, TEXAS IN 1834 AND WENT INTO THE STEAMBOAT AND MERCANTILE BUSINESS WITH THOMAS HULING AND HENRY MILLARD.

GLASSCOCK ALSO FOUGHT IN THE TEXAS REVOLUTION.

MILLARD WENT ON TO FOUND BEAUMONT, TX.

A TOWN AND A COUNTY IN DIFFERENT PARTS OF TEXAS WERE NAMED AFTER GEORGE GLASSCOCK.

GEORGE W. GLASSCOCK, A PROSPEROUS BUSINESSMAN, MOVED WITH HIS WIFE TO CENTRAL TEXAS IN 1840. WHEN WILLIAMSON COUNTY WAS ORGANIZED IN 1848, MR. GLASSCOCK DONATED 172 ACRES FOR THE COUNTY SEAT.

THE TOWN WAS NAMED IN HIS HONOR—

Georgetown.

HE ALSO BUILT A MILL FOR GRINDING WHEAT AND CORN.

GLASSCOCK WENT ON TO REPRESENT WILLIAMSON COUNTY IN THE STATE HOUSE.

OUR FIRST SENATORS

BEFORE THE 17th AMENDMENT TOOK EFFECT IN 1913, UNITED STATES SENATORS WERE ELECTED BY STATE LEGIS-LATURES.

THE U.S. CAPITOL IN 1846.

TEXAS BECAME A STATE ON DECEMBER 29, 1845. SEVEN WEEKS LATER THE TEXAS STATE LEGISLATURE ELECTED OUR FIRST TWO SENATORS:

SAM HOUSTON

THOMAS JEFFERSON RUSK FOUGHT FOR A SOUTHERN ROUTE THROUGH TEXAS FOR THE TRANS-CONTINENTAL RAILROAD.

HE WAS ELECTED PRESIDENT PRO TEMPORE OF THE SENATE IN 1857.

SAM SERVED FOURTEEN YEARS. HE WAS VILIFIED AS A TRAITOR TO THE SOUTH AFTER HE VOTED AGAINST THE KANSAS-NEBRASKA BILL WHICH ALLOWED FOR THE EXPANSION OF SLAVERY.

The Swiss Merchant

HENRY ROSENBERG CAME FROM SWITZERLAND TO TEXAS IN 1843 AT THE AGE OF 19. HE CLERKED IN A DRY GOODS STORE IN **GALVESTON** FOR $8 A WEEK.

AFTER THE OWNER LEFT THE COUNTRY, HENRY TOOK OVER THE BUSINESS. BY 1850 HE HAD BUILT IT INTO THE **LARGEST** MERCANTILE ENTERPRISE IN TEXAS.

do Santa Fe Rail Road

ROSENBERG · HOUSTON
EAST BERNARD
GALVE

MR. ROSENBERG ORGANIZED A BANK IN 1874. HE ALSO RAN GALVESTON'S HARBOR AND TROLLEY LINE.

THE TOWN OF ROSENBERG, SOUTHWEST OF HOUSTON, WAS NAMED AFTER HIM BECAUSE HE CHAIRED A RAILROAD THAT WENT THROUGH THE VILLAGE.

Fancy Squirts

ONE OF THE MOST SUCCESSFUL BUSINESSMEN IN 19th CENTURY TEXAS WAS A SWISS IMMIGRANT LIVING IN **GALVESTON** NAMED **HENRY ROSENBERG.**

TWICE MARRIED, HIS WIVE'S DIED WITHOUT HAVING CHILDREN. HE DIED IN 1893 AT THE AGE OF 69 LEAVING AN UNUSUAL WILL WHICH BENEFITED THE CITY HE LOVED SO MUCH.

HIS ESTATE FUNDED THE CONSTRUCTION OF A LIBRARY, A YMCA, A WOMEN'S HOME, A TEXAS HEROES MONUMENT, AN ORPHANAGE, CHURCHES, AND SCHOOLS.

HE STIPULATED THAT $30,000 BE USED TO BUILD AT LEAST TEN DRINKING FOUNTAINS "FOR MAN AND BEAST." SHOWN HERE ARE SOME OF THE 17 "ROSENBERG" FOUNTAINS IN GALVESTON.

THE FIRST COWBOY STRIKE

IN TEXAS TOOK PLACE WHEN 325 COWBOYS CEASED WORK IN THE PANHANDLE FROM MARCH 24 TO APRIL 3, 1883.

TOM HARRIS HELD A MEETING IN A DUGOUT IN **TASCOSA** WHERE STRIKERS DEMANDED A MINIMUM OF $50 A MONTH FOR COWHANDS AND COOKS, AND $75 MONTHLY FOR TRAIL BOSSES.

THE COWBOYS SUCCEEDED IN GETTING A RAISE FROM $1.18 A DAY TO $1.68 PER DAY WHICH AMOUNTS TO $50.40 FOR 30 DAYS' WORK.

From Gunslinger to Lawyer

JOHN WESLEY HARDIN, THE NOTORIOUS GUNSLINGER FROM BONHAM, WAS CONVICTED IN 1878 OF ONE OF HIS FORTY-FOUR MURDERS.

WHILE DOING A 25-YEAR STRETCH AT HUNTSVILLE STATE PRISON HARDIN STUDIED ALGEBRA, THEOLOGY, AND LAW.

PARDONED BY THE GOVERNOR IN 1894, HARDIN PASSED THE BAR EXAM AND OPENED A LAW PRACTICE IN GONZALES. BUT HIS BAD TEMPER RUINED HIS BUSINESS. SO, HE MOVED TO EL PASO, ADOPTED A MR. NICE-GUY ATTITUDE, AND WAS MORE SUCCESSFUL

THE BAKER

GROWING UP IN BELGIUM, EDWARD WELTENS DEVELOPED A TALENT AS A BAKER. AROUND 1881 HE WORKED HIS WAY ACROSS THE ATLANTIC AS A CHEF ON A LINER.

HE SETTLED IN **SAN ANTONIO** AND BECAME A PASTRY CHEF AT THE MENGER HOTEL. HE DREAMED OF HAVING HIS OWN BAKERY.

BY THE OUTBREAK OF THE SPANISH-AMERICAN WAR IN 1898, EDWARD HAD SAVED ENOUGH MONEY TO OPEN HIS OWN BAKERY.

WHILE TEDDY ROOSEVELT WAS TRAINING HIS ROUGH RIDERS ON THE OLD FAIRGROUNDS, IT WAS MR. WELTENS WHO SUPPLIED THEM WITH BREAD AND PASTRIES.

WELTENS BAKERY
FINE PASTRIES

The Crack-Shot Cartoonist

ADOLPH "AD" TOEPPERWEIN OF BOERNE WAS THE BEST MARKSMAN AND TRICK SHOT GUNMAN OF THE EARLY 1900s.

HE SET 14 WORLD RECORDS DURING THE 36 YEARS THAT HE TOURED FOR THE WINCHESTER ARMS CO. HE OUTSHOT SUCH STARS AS BUFFALO BILL CODY.

AT THE AGE OF 20, IN 1889, AD GOT A JOB AS A CARTOONIST FOR THE SAN ANTONIO *EXPRESS*.

THIS GAVE HIM AN IDEA FOR A TRICK SHOT ROUTINE. FROM A DISTANCE OF 30 YARDS HE "SHOT" A PICTURE ON A PIECE OF TIN USING ABOUT 300 BULLETS.

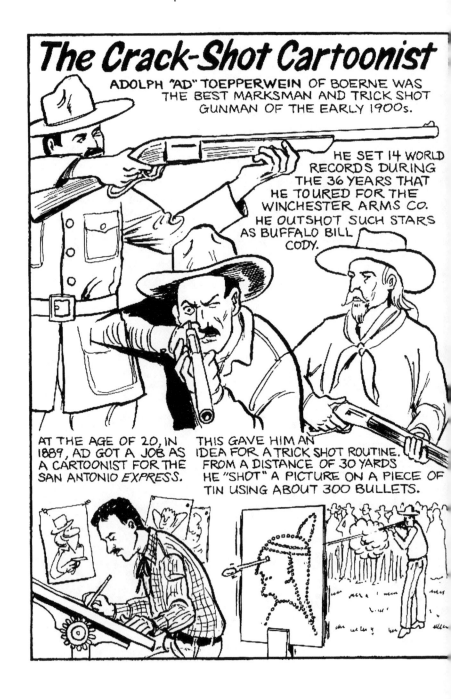

CORRINE MAE GRIFFITH WAS BORN IN HILL COUNTY, TEXAS AROUND 1895. SHE ATTENDED THE UNIVERSITY OF TEXAS FOR ONE SEMESTER IN 1912.

FOUR YEARS LATER, A FELLOW TEXAN, MOVIE DIRECTOR KING VIDOR GOT HER INTO THE MOVIE BUSINESS. AT FIRST SHE MADE $5 A WEEK.

BECAUSE OF HER DELICATE FEATURES SHE BECAME KNOWN AS THE

Orchid of the Silver Screen.

CORRINE WAS ONE OF THE MOST POPULAR MOVIE STARS IN THE 1920s. SHE ALSO MADE MILLIONS BY INVESTING IN REAL ESTATE.

SHE STARRED IN THE LADY IN ERMINE, THE GARDEN OF EDEN, AND OTHERS. SHE DIED IN 1979.

PLAY BALL!

BASEBALL WAS PLAYED IN TEXAS AS FAR BACK AS 1861. THE EARLIEST KNOWN GAME TO BE REPORTED OCCURRED IN 1867.

ON SAN JACINTO DAY, APRIL 21, 1867, THE STONE-WALLS OF HOUSTON WERE CLOBBERED BY THE R.E. LEES OF GALVESTON, 35-2.

AN AMATEUR CLUB FROM NEW ORLEANS (ALSO CALLED THE R.E. LEES) BARNSTORMED ACROSS TEXAS ON A STAGECOACH IN 1877, PLAYING TEAMS IN DALLAS, AUSTIN, AND WACO.

HONEST JOHN McCLOSKEY

BROUGHT A PROFESSIONAL BASEBALL TEAM, THE JOPLIN (MISSOURI) INDEPENDENTS, TO TEXAS IN 1887 AND LINED UP GAMES WITH LOCAL CLUBS IN FOURTEEN CITIES.

McCLOSKEY WAS IMPRESSED BY THE TEXANS' ENTHUSIASM FOR THE SPORT.

McCLOSKEY HELD A MEETING ON DECEMBER 15, 1887 IN AUSTIN TO ORGANIZE A "STATE BASE BALL LEAGUE." REPRESENTATIVES FROM DALLAS, HOUSTON, FORT WORTH, AND NEW ORLEANS ATTENDED.

GALVESTON AND SAN ANTONIO SENT LETTERS OF APPLICATION. THIS WAS THE BEGINNING OF THE

TEXAS LEAGUE.

ONE OF THE GREATEST CATCHERS AND POWER HITTERS IN THE OLD **NEGRO BASEBALL LEAGUES** WAS **LOUIS "TOP" SANTOP.**

HE WAS BORN LOUIS SANTOP LOFTIN IN **TYLER, TEXAS** IN 1890.

LOUIS DROPPED HIS LAST NAME IN 1909 WHEN HE BEGAN HIS PROFESSIONAL BALL CAREER WITH THE **FORT WORTH WONDERS.**

IN A CAREER THAT LASTED UNTIL 1926, "TOP" SANTOP PLAYED FOR THE PHILADELPHIA GIANTS, LINCOLN STARS, HILLDALE (A BLACK TEAM IN PHILADELPHIA), AND OTHERS.

WHILE PLAYING FOR HILLDALE IN THE 1920s HE EARNED $500 A WEEK.

MR. SANTOP DIED IN 1942.

Women Playing Hardball

MOST OF AMERICA'S BASEBALL PLAYERS WERE IN THE ARMED FORCES DURING WORLD WAR II. SO, IN 1942, PHILIP K. WRIGLEY, OWNER OF THE CHICAGO CUBS, ORGANIZED THE ALL-AMERICAN GIRLS PROFESSIONAL BASEBALL LEAGUE.

AMONG THE PLAYERS FROM TEXAS WAS ALVA JO FISCHER OF SAN ANTONIO, A PITCHER, SHORTSTOP, AND TOP-NOTCH HITTER FOR THE ROCKFORD PEACHES (1945) AND MUSKEGON LASSIES (1947-49).

THE TEAMS WERE LOCATED IN THE UPPER MIDWEST.

WISCONSIN

MICHIGAN
· MUSKEGON
  LASSIES
GRAND RAPIDS
· CHICKS

RACINE
BELLES ·
KENOSHA COMETS ·

ROCKFORD
PEACHES
· SOUTH BEND
BLUE SOX ·
PEORIA
REDWINGS
·
ILLINOIS
FORT WAYNE
DAISIES

· SPRINGFIELD
SALLIES
INDIANA

MARIE MAHONEY OF HOUSTON PLAYED OUT FIELD FOR THE SOUTH BEND BLUE SOX (1947) AND THE FORT WAYNE DAISIES (1948).

THE LEAGUE FOLDED IN 1954.

THE FIRST FRONTIER FORT

IN TEXAS BUILT BY THE **U.S. ARMY** WAS FORT **MARTIN SCOTT.** ESTABLISHED ON DEC. 8, 1848 IT WAS NAMED AFTER A BREVET LIEUTENANT COLONEL WHO WAS KILLED A YEAR EARLIER AT THE BATTLE OF MOLINO DEL REY IN MEXICO.

LOCATED 2½ MILES SOUTHEAST OF FREDERICKSBURG, ITS MISSION WAS TO PROTECT TRAVELERS ON THE ROAD BETWEEN SAN ANTONIO AND FREDERICKSBURG FROM THE COMANCHES.

FORT MARTIN SCOTT WAS MANNED ONLY OCCASIONALLY AFTER 1852. CONFEDERATE TROOPS USED IT DURING THE CIVIL WAR. IT WAS ABANDONED FOR GOOD ON DEC. 28, 1866.

ONE OF THE EARLY FRONTIER FORTS IN TEXAS,

FORT INGE,

WAS ESTABLISHED IN 1849 BY U.S. TROOPS UNDER CAPTAIN SIDNEY BURBANK AND NAMED FOR LIEUTENANT ZEBULON INGE WHO WAS KILLED IN THE MEXICAN WAR.

SITUATED AT THE BASE OF "MOUNT" INGE IN UVALDE COUNTY, THE GARRISON'S MAIN PURPOSE WAS TO PROTECT TRAVELERS BETWEEN SAN ANTONIO AND EL PASO.

SOLDIERS FROM FORT INGE SUCH AS CORPORAL JOHN BOYDEN AND SERGEANT WILLIAM P. LEVERETT FOUGHT MANY BATTLES WITH HOSTILE COMANCHES.

FORT INGE WAS ABANDONED IN 1869.

FORT EWELL

WAS ESTABLISHED IN 1852 ALONG THE NUECES RIVER IN LASALLE COUNTY BY A REGIMENT OF THE MOUNTED RIFLES. ITS MISSION WAS TO PROTECT TRAVELERS ON THE SAN ANTONIO-LAREDO ROAD.

UNDER THE SUPERVISION OF LT. COL. WILLIAM LORING, THE SOLDIERS MADE THE ADOBE BRICKS AND PUT UP THE TEMPORARY BUILDINGS.

IT WAS NAMED FOR CAPTAIN RICHARD EWELL, A VETERAN OF THE MEXICAN WAR.

FORT CIBOLO,

SPANISH FOR *BUFFALO*, WAS A PRIVATE FORT BUILT IN 1856 NEAR MARFA, PRESIDIO COUNTY BY MILTON FAVER, THE FIRST ANGLO-AMERICAN CATTLE RANCHER IN THE REGION.

FAVER USED PEACHES FROM A NEARBY ORCHARD TO MAKE HIS OWN BRANDY.

THE U.S. ARMY GAVE HIM A CANNON AND GARRISONED TROOPS THERE.

FAVER BECAME THE FIRST LARGE-SCALE RANCHER IN THE BIG BEND AREA WHEN HIS HERD GREW FROM THE ORIGINAL 300 HEAD TO OVER 10,000.

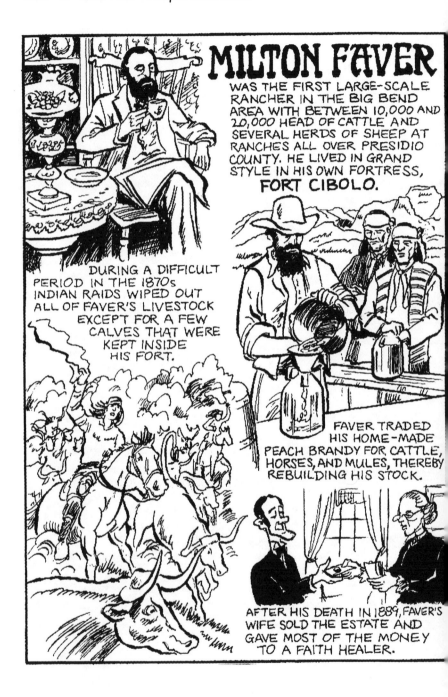

MILTON FAVER

WAS THE FIRST LARGE-SCALE RANCHER IN THE BIG BEND AREA WITH BETWEEN 10,000 AND 20,000 HEAD OF CATTLE AND SEVERAL HERDS OF SHEEP AT RANCHES ALL OVER PRESIDIO COUNTY. HE LIVED IN GRAND STYLE IN HIS OWN FORTRESS, **FORT CIBOLO.**

DURING A DIFFICULT PERIOD IN THE 1870s INDIAN RAIDS WIPED OUT ALL OF FAVER'S LIVESTOCK EXCEPT FOR A FEW CALVES THAT WERE KEPT INSIDE HIS FORT.

FAVER TRADED HIS HOME-MADE PEACH BRANDY FOR CATTLE, HORSES, AND MULES, THEREBY REBUILDING HIS STOCK.

AFTER HIS DEATH IN 1889, FAVER'S WIFE SOLD THE ESTATE AND GAVE MOST OF THE MONEY TO A FAITH HEALER.

HORACE RANDAL WAS LIVING IN SAN AUGUSTINE, TX IN 1849 WHEN HE RECEIVED AN APPOINTMENT TO THE UNITED STATES MILITARY ACADEMY, MAKING HIM

THE FIRST TEXAN AT WEST POINT.

AFTER GRADUATING IN 1854, LIEUTENANT RANDAL WAS ASSIGNED TO FRONTIER DUTY IN NEW MEXICO, THEN EL PASO, AND (SHOWN HERE) FORT DAVIS, TEXAS.

GENERAL RANDAL

ON THE EVE OF THE CIVIL WAR, FEB. 27, 1861, LT. HORACE RANDAL RESIGNED FROM THE U.S. ARMY. A MONTH LATER HE WAS MADE A COLONEL IN THE 28th CONFEDERATE CAVALRY. HE SERVED IN LOUISIANA AND ARKANSAS.

HE MARRIED NANNIE TAYLOR AT MARSHALL, TX IN 1862. THEY HAD A SON, HORACE, JR.

TWO YEARS LATER, ON APRIL 30, 1864, GENERAL RANDAL WAS KILLED IN ARKANSAS AT THE BATTLE OF JENKIN'S FERRY.

HE WAS BURIED IN MARSHALL IN A GRAVE THAT HAD NO MARKER UNTIL 1893.

RANDALL COUNTY,

SITUATED IN THE TEXAS PANHANDLE, WAS CREATED IN 1876 AND NAMED FOR HORACE RANDAL, A CONFEDERATE GENERAL.

FOR CENTURIES PUEBLO INDIANS, FROM WHAT IS NOW NEW MEXICO, TREKKED HERE TO HUNT BUFFALO.

AMARILLO
LAKE TANGLEWOOD
CANYON
CLETA
BUFFALO LAKE
OGG

IN 1876 CHARLES GOODNIGHT DROVE THE FIRST HERD OF CATTLE INTO RANDALL COUNTY—1,600 HEAD. RANCHING HAS REMAINED THE AREA'S MAIN INDUSTRY.

GOODNIGHT'S BROTHER-IN-LAW, LEIGH DYER, BECAME THE COUNTY'S FIRST SETTLER IN 1877.

AT THE OUTBREAK OF THE CIVIL WAR IN 1861 STATE SENATOR SAM BELL MAXEY LEFT OFFICE TO RECRUIT MEN FOR THE CONFEDERATE ARMY. GENERAL MAXEY TRAINED HIS TROOPS AT FORT BEN FRANKLIN IN DELTA COUNTY, AND THEY COMPRISED

the Texas 9th Infantry Regiment.

THE BONNIE BLUE FLAG

ON JANUARY 1, 1862 THE 9th REGIMENT LEFT TEXAS AND HEADED EAST. THEY FOUGHT IN MANY BATTLES INCLUDING VICKSBURG, CHICKAMAUGA, SHILOH, ATLANTA, AND MURFREESBORO.

RUNAWAY SLAVES

THERE WAS NO UNDERGROUND RAILROAD TO HELP SLAVES ESCAPE FROM TEXAS IN THE EARLY 19th CENTURY. HERE RUNAWAYS WERE ON THEIR OWN.

SOME MADE IT TO THE GULF COAST AND STOWED AWAY ON SHIPS BOUND FOR FOREIGN OR NORTHERN PORTS.

A FEW JOINED INDIAN TRIBES. BECAUSE OF THEIR KNOWLEDGE OF WHITE SOCIETY, SOME EX-SLAVES ACTED AS TRANSLATORS. OTHERS HELPED PLAN AND DIRECT RAIDING PARTIES.

Wild Cat and the Escape

THE MAIN DESTINATION FOR SLAVES ESCAPING FROM TEXAS WAS MEXICO. ONE OF THE MOST SENSATIONAL MASS ESCAPES FROM TEXAS OCCURRED IN 1849 WHEN A SEMINOLE CHIEF NAMED WILD CAT LED OVER 150 BLACKS AND INDIANS ACROSS THE DESERT TO MEXICO.

BY 1851 ABOUT 3,000 SLAVES HAD CROSSED THE RIO GRANDE TO FREEDOM, FOLLOWED BY ANOTHER THOUSAND OVER THE NEXT FOUR YEARS.

THE QUILT CODE

BEFORE THE CIVIL WAR, SLAVES IN THE U.S. WERE DENIED AN EDUCATION LEST THEY GET IDEAS ABOUT FREEDOM. BUT, OWNERS WERE PLEASED WHEN THEIR SLAVES TOOK UP CRAFTS SUCH AS QUILT MAKING.

UNBEKNOWNST TO THE OWNERS, THE QUILTS CONTAINED SECRET CODES WHICH AIDED SLAVES IN THEIR ESCAPE TO FREEDOM.

CODED QUILTS LEFT OUT "TO DRY:"

MONKEY WRENCH
GATHER ALL TOOLS
YOU MIGHT NEED
ON JOURNEY TO FREEDOM.

WAGON WHEEL
YOU WILL BE
TRAVELLING
BY WAGON.

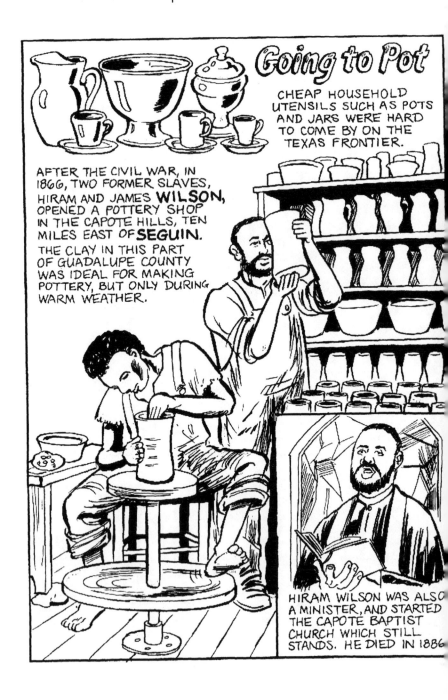

Going to Pot

CHEAP HOUSEHOLD UTENSILS SUCH AS POTS AND JARS WERE HARD TO COME BY ON THE TEXAS FRONTIER.

AFTER THE CIVIL WAR, IN 1866, TWO FORMER SLAVES, HIRAM AND JAMES **WILSON,** OPENED A POTTERY SHOP IN THE CAPOTE HILLS, TEN MILES EAST OF **SEGUIN.** THE CLAY IN THIS PART OF GUADALUPE COUNTY WAS IDEAL FOR MAKING POTTERY, BUT ONLY DURING WARM WEATHER.

HIRAM WILSON WAS ALSO A MINISTER, AND STARTED THE CAPOTE BAPTIST CHURCH WHICH STILL STANDS. HE DIED IN 1886.

MATTHEW GAINES

WAS BORN A SLAVE IN 1840 IN LOUISIANA. HE LEARNED TO READ FROM BOOKS SMUGGLED TO HIM BY A WHITE BOY WHO LIVED ON THE SAME PLANTATION.

MATTHEW WAS EVENTUALLY SOLD TO A PLANTER IN ROBERTSON COUNTY, TEXAS. GAINES ESCAPED IN 1863 BUT WAS CAPTURED NEAR FORT McKAVETT.

AFTER THE CIVIL WAR GAINES SETTLED IN WASHINGTON COUNTY, TEXAS WHERE HE BECAME A MINISTER. IN 1869 HE WAS ELECTED TO THE STATE SENATE.

SENATOR GAINES ADVOCATED PRISON REFORM AND EDUCATION FOR AFRICAN AMERICANS.

AMID THE IMPEACHMENT

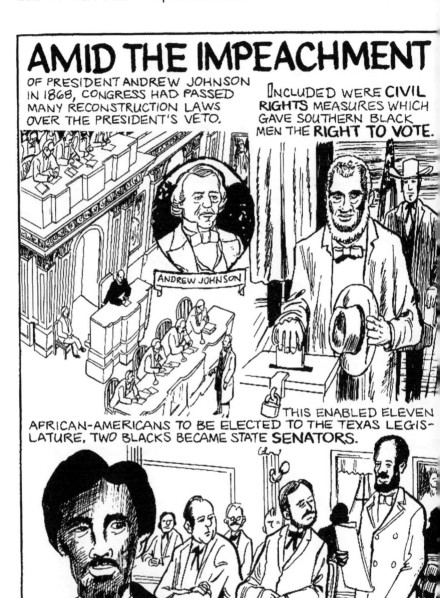

OF PRESIDENT ANDREW JOHNSON IN 1868, CONGRESS HAD PASSED MANY RECONSTRUCTION LAWS OVER THE PRESIDENT'S VETO.

INCLUDED WERE **CIVIL RIGHTS** MEASURES WHICH GAVE SOUTHERN BLACK MEN THE **RIGHT TO VOTE.**

ANDREW JOHNSON

THIS ENABLED ELEVEN AFRICAN-AMERICANS TO BE ELECTED TO THE TEXAS LEGISLATURE. TWO BLACKS BECAME STATE **SENATORS.**

MATTHEW GAINES OF BURTON, WASHINGTON COUNTY. & GEORGE THOMPSON RUBY OF GALVESTON

SUL ROSS STATE
UNIVERSITY IN **ALPINE** WAS NAMED AFTER A GOVERNOR OF TEXAS WHO, AS A COLLEGE STUDENT, FOUGHT INDIANS DURING HIS SUMMER VACATION.

LAWRENCE SULLIVAN ROSS
WAS BORN IN 1839. HIS FATHER, SHAPLEY PRINCE ROSS, WAS THE U.S. AGENT AT THE BRAZOS INDIAN RESERVATION NEAR WACO. YOUNG "SUL" ROSS ATTENDED BAYLOR UNIVERSITY FOR A WHILE.

DURING A SUMMER VACATION HE LED A COMPANY OF INDIANS FROM THE RESERVATION ON A CAMPAIGN AGAINST HOSTILE COMANCHES.

IN 1859 SUL ROSS JOINED THE TEXAS RANGERS.

LAWRENCE SULLIVAN ROSS

GRADUATED FROM WESLEYAN UNIVERSITY IN FLORENCE, ALABAMA IN 1859 AND WAS COMMISSIONED A CAPTAIN OF TEXAS RANGERS AT THE AGE OF 21.
SOON HE LED 120 MEN TO A LARGE COMANCHE TOWN IN HARDEMAN COUNTY AND RECAPTURED CYNTHIA ANN PARKER.

SUL ROSS QUIT THE RANGERS IN FEBRUARY 1861, THEN MARRIED LIZZIE TINSLEY. MEANWHILE, THE CIVIL WAR HAD STARTED.

SUL ENLISTED IN THE CONFEDERATE ARMY AS A PRIVATE. HE QUICKLY ROSE TO THE RANK OF BRIGADIER GENERAL IN COMMAND OF A TEXAS BRIGADE.

AFTER THE CIVIL WAR, CONFEDERATE GENERAL **SUL ROSS** ENTERED POLITICS AS SHERIFF OF McLELLAN COUNTY. IN 1886 HE WAS ELECTED THE 17th GOVERNOR OF TEXAS. REELECTED IN 1888, HIS ADMINISTRATION ENJOYED LOW TAXES, A RELATIVELY SAFE FRONTIER, INCREASED AID TO EDUCATION, AND COMPLETION OF THE STATE CAPITOL IN AUSTIN. ROSS' TENURE WAS REGARDED AS *THE ERA OF GOOD FEELING.*

ON LEAVING AUSTIN IN 1891, SUL ROSS WAS SELECTED AS PRESIDENT OF THE AGRICULTURAL AND MECHANICAL COLLEGE OF TEXAS (TEXAS A & M). UNDER HIS LEADERSHIP ENROLLMENT INCREASED REQUIRING AN EXTENSIVE CONSTRUCTION PROGRAM. GOVERNOR ROSS DIED IN 1898.

GOVERNOR RICHARD COKE SPOKE AT THE DEDICATION AND OPENING OF THE AGRICULTURAL AND MECHANICAL COLLEGE OF TEXAS NEAR **BRYAN** ON OCTOBER 4, 1876. MANDATED BY LAW, FINANCED BY TAXES, AND BUILT ON PUBLIC LAND, IT WAS

the First Land-Grant College in Texas.

...LET HONOR BE YOUR GUIDE.

ONLY SIX STUDENTS REGISTERED DURING THE FIRST DAYS OF ENROLLMENT. BY THE END OF THE FIRST TERM THERE WERE FORTY-EIGHT. EACH STUDENT HAD TO PURCHASE SEVEN COLLARS, SEVEN SHIRTS, TWO UNIFORMS, AND A FORAGE CAP.

DURING ITS FIRST FEW YEARS, THE COLLEGE HAD NO BATHING FACILITIES.

An Innovative College

THE AGRICULTURAL & MECHANICAL COLLEGE OF TEXAS, NEAR BRYAN, WAS AUTHORIZED TO TEACH AGRICULTURAL AND MECHANICAL ARTS—SUBJECTS RARELY TAUGHT ELSEWHERE.
THESE INCLUDED WOODWORKING, SURVEYING, AND MACHINERY.

CADET TEMPLE HOUSTON, SON OF GENERAL SAM HOUSTON, WAS PART OF A&M'S FIRST CLASS IN 1876.

WHILE OTHER COLLEGES WERE STARTING SOCIAL CLUBS AND FRATERNITIES, NONE WERE ENCOURAGED OR DEVELOPED AT A&M. INSTEAD, THE STUDENT BODY BECAME A SINGLE FRATERNITY KNOWN AS THE **CORPS OF CADETS.**

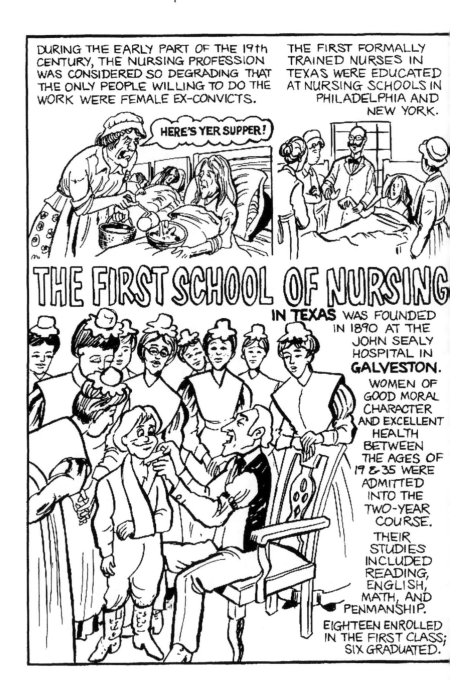

Liz the Librarian

ELIZABETH HOWARD WEST, A NATIVE OF MISSISSIPPI, CAME TO TEXAS IN 1911 TO BE THE ARCHIVIST OF THE TEXAS STATE LIBRARY.

FROM 1915 TO 1918 MS. WEST WORKED IN THE CARNEGIE LIBRARY IN **SAN ANTONIO.**

ELIZABETH BECAME THE FIRST WOMAN TO HEAD A DEPARTMENT IN TEXAS STATE GOVERNMENT WHEN SHE WAS NAMED **STATE LIBRARIAN** AT AUSTIN IN 1918.

SHE STIMULATED THE TEXAS FREE LIBRARY SYSTEM AND STARTED SERVICES FOR THE BLIND.

DURING THE 1930s MS. WEST DID RESEARCH IN SPAIN FOR THE LIBRARY OF CONGRESS. SHE DIED IN FLORIDA IN 1948.

THE ARANSAS PASS LIGHTHOUSE

BEGAN OPERATING IN 1857 AFTER THREE YEARS UNDER CONSTRUCTION.

EARLY IN THE CIVIL WAR BOTH NORTHERN AND SOUTHERN SOLDIERS USED IT AS A LOOKOUT TO SPY ON NAVAL MANEUVERS IN THE GULF.

JUST BEFORE CHRISTMAS, 1862 THE CONFEDERATES SET EXPLOSIVES AND BLEW OFF THE TOP TO PREVENT THE YANKEES FROM USING IT DURING AN EXPECTED INVASION OF TEXAS.

THE LIGHTHOUSE WAS FIXED IN 1867 AND FUNCTIONED UNTIL 1952.

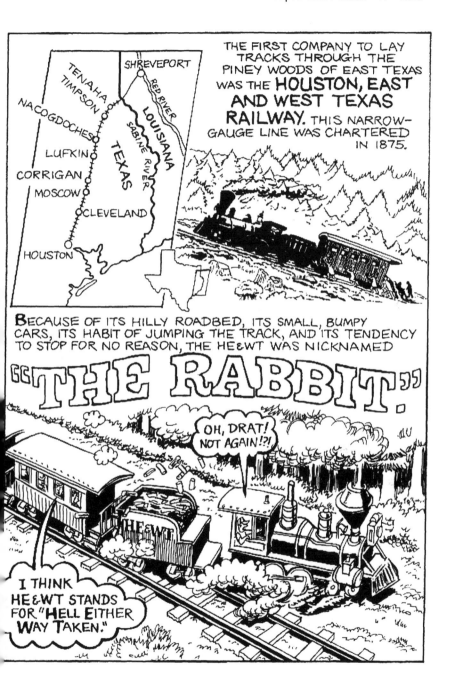

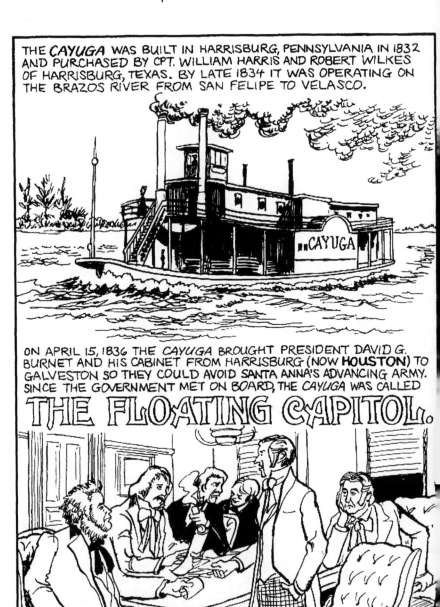

THE *CAYUGA* WAS BUILT IN HARRISBURG, PENNSYLVANIA IN 1832 AND PURCHASED BY CPT. WILLIAM HARRIS AND ROBERT WILKES OF HARRISBURG, TEXAS. BY LATE 1834 IT WAS OPERATING ON THE BRAZOS RIVER FROM SAN FELIPE TO VELASCO.

ON APRIL 15, 1836 THE *CAYUGA* BROUGHT PRESIDENT DAVID G. BURNET AND HIS CABINET FROM HARRISBURG (NOW **HOUSTON**) TO GALVESTON SO THEY COULD AVOID SANTA ANNA'S ADVANCING ARMY. SINCE THE GOVERNMENT MET ON BOARD, THE *CAYUGA* WAS CALLED **THE FLOATING CAPITOL.**

THE ELISSA

WAS LAUNCHED IN 1877 AT THE ALEXANDER HALL & CO. SHIPYARD IN ABERDEEN, SCOTLAND. THIS 400 TON, 150 FOOT SHIP WAS MADE OF WROUGHT IRON. COMMERCIALLY ACTIVE FOR ALMOST A CENTURY, SHE MADE SEVERAL STOPS IN GALVESTON.

BY THE 1960s THE *ELISSA* HAD FALLEN INTO THE HANDS OF SMUGGLERS ON THE MEDITERRANEAN SEA.

IN 1975 THE GALVESTON HISTORICAL FOUNDATION PURCHASED THE OLD SHIP AND RESTORED HER.

BERTHED AT GALVESTON'S PIER 21, THE *ELISSA* IS THE OLDEST, SEAWORTHY, IRON SAILING SHIP IN THE WORLD.

WILLIAM HENRY HAMBLEN

WAS RANCHING NEAR **WAYSIDE** IN THE **PALO DURO CANYON** DURING THE 1890s.

AT THE TIME, A PERSON GOING FROM SILVERTON TO CLAUDE HAD TO MAKE A 120 MILE TREK AROUND THE CANYON. ON HIS OWN, BILL CUT A ROAD ACROSS THE CANYON.

AMARILLO
CLAUDE
DIRT TRAIL
HAMBLEN'S CRUDE ROAD
WAYSIDE
PALO DURO
DIRT TRAIL
SILVERTON

FOLLOWING OLD INDIAN TRAILS, THIS SIX-MILE ROAD CUT THE TRIP TO CLAUDE IN HALF.

HOWEVER, THE ROAD WAS STEEP AND DANGEROUS, SO MR. HAMBLEN VOWED TO HAVE A BETTER ROAD CONSTRUCTED.

THE PALO DURO HIGHWAY

WILL HAMBLEN HAD BUILT A CRUDE, UNSAFE ROAD ACROSS PALO DURO CANYON IN THE 1890s. OVER THE NEXT THREE DECADES HE CAMPAIGNED FOR A BETTER ROAD.

THEN, IN 1928 BILL WAS ELECTED COMMISSIONER OF ARMSTRONG COUNTY. WITHIN TWO YEARS AN IMPROVED GRAVEL ROAD WAS COMPLETED ACROSS AN OLD BUFFALO TRAIL. THE STATE MADE IT A HARD-SURFACE HIGHWAY IN 1954.

TODAY STATE ROUTE 207 THROUGH THE CANYON STILL BEARS THE NAME IT WAS GIVEN IN 1930— **HAMBLEN DRIVE.**

LEGEND SAYS THE COMANCHES SACRIFICED A GIRL'S DOLL WITH BLUE-JAY FEATHERS SO THE GREAT SPIRIT WOULD END THEIR STARVATION.

THE ASHES WERE STREWN TO THE WINDS. THE NEXT DAY BLUE FLOWERS APPEARED.

MANY YEARS LATER THESE FLOWERS WERE CALLED BLUEBONNETS BECAUSE THEY RESEMBLED THE BONNETS WORN BY PIONEER WOMEN.

THE BLUEBONNET

(*LUPINUS SUBCARNOSIS*) WAS PROCLAIMED THE **STATE FLOWER** OF TEXAS BY THE LEGISLATURE ON MAR. 7, 1901. THE FLOWER BLOOMS DURING THE MONTH OF APRIL.

BLUEBONNET TRAIL

THERE ARE BLUEBONNET TRAILS THROUGHOUT TEXAS BUT ONE OF THE OLDEST IS AT **ENNIS** WITH OVER 40 MILES OF WELL MARKED TRAILS AROUND ELLIS COUNTY.

DANGEROUS-S-S-SNAKES

SIXTEEN SPECIES OF POISONOUS SNAKES LIVE IN TEXAS AND OVER HALF ARE RATTLERS. EACH COUNTY HAS AT LEAST ONE SPECIE.

THE LARGEST VENOM-PACKER IS THE **WESTERN DIAMONDBACK RATTLE-SNAKE** (CROTALUS ATROX). THE AVERAGE LENGTH IS 4½ FEET.

THE MOST COLORFUL OF THE POISONOUS SERPENTS IS THE **TEXAS CORAL SNAKE** (MICRURUS FULVIUS TENERE). ITS USUAL LENGTH IS 2½ FEET.

THE SMALLEST AND LEAST DANGEROUS IS THE **WESTERN PIGMY RATTLESNAKE** (SISTRURUS MILIARIUS STRECKERI). IT USUALLY GROWS TO ABOUT EIGHTEEN INCHES LONG.

Beneath the Lone Star

TEXAS HAS OVER **3,000** MAPPED **CAVES**. MOST ARE LOCATED IN **CENTRAL AND WEST TEXAS**. AS EARLY AS 1800 THE CURIOUS AND ADVENTUROUS WERE EXPLORING TEXAS CAVES WITH LANTERNS AND TORCHES.

CASCADE CAVERNS NEAR BOERNE WAS THE FIRST COMMERCIAL CAVE IN TEXAS. IT OPENED FOR VISITORS IN 1932.

OTHER COMMERCIAL CAVES INCLUDE: THE CAVERNS OF SONORA; LONGHORN CAVERN NEAR BURNET; INNER SPACE CAVERN, GEORGETOWN; NATURAL BRIDGE CAVERNS, 17 MILES WEST OF NEW BRAUNFELS; AND WONDER WORLD, SAN MARCOS.

POWELL'S CAVE,

IN **MENARD COUNTY**, IS THE **LARGEST** CAVE IN TEXAS WITH OVER 38,000 FEET OF MAPPED PASSAGES. IT WAS FIRST CALLED **JACKPIT**, FROM THE SLANG TERM *JACK*, MEANING **SILVER**. ALLEGEDLY JAMES BOWIE HID A LOAD OF SILVER HERE.

POWELL'S CAVE IS A SYSTEM OF THREE CAVERNS WITH SEPARATE ENTRANCES. THE CAVE HAS A DRY UPPER LEVEL WHILE A STREAM FLOWS THROUGH THE LOWER LEVEL.

Yuletide Places

THE **CHRISTMAS MOUNTAINS** ARE LOCATED IN THE SOUTHERN PART OF **BREWSTER COUNTY** JUST OUTSIDE BIG BEND NATIONAL PARK. THEIR AVERAGE ELEVATION IS 3,600 FEET.

CHRISTMAS MOUNTAINS

WACO•

CHRISTMAS •CREEK

A GROUP OF SURVEYORS CAMPED BESIDE A STREAM NEAR WACO (ACTUALLY IN LIMESTONE COUNTY) ON DECEMBER 25, 1885, SO THEY CALLED IT **CHRISTMAS CREEK.**

GOOD OL' ST. NICHOLAS

ST. NICHOLAS WAS THE BISHOP OF MYRA, TURKEY IN THE 4th CENTURY. HE'S USUALLY SHOWN HOLDING 3 BAGS OF GOLD THAT SYMBOL- IZE THE DOWRIES HE GAVE TO THE DAUGHTERS OF A POOR MERCHANT.

HE SECRETLY TOSSED BAGS OF GOLD THROUGH THE WINDOWS OF THE THREE SISTERS. THEREAFTER, ST. NICK WAS GIVEN CREDIT FOR UNEXPECTED GIFTS.

ONE VERSION OF THIS STORY CLAIMS THAT ONE OF THE BAGS FELL INTO A STOCKING THAT WAS HANGING TO DRY.

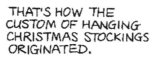

THAT'S HOW THE CUSTOM OF HANGING CHRISTMAS STOCKINGS ORIGINATED.

MONEYLENDERS IN ITALY ADOPTED NICH- OLAS AS THEIR PATRON SAINT AND PLACED THREE GOLD BALLS OVER THEIR PLACES OF BUSINESS.

IN AMERICA THIS SIGN BECAME THE SYMBOL FOR **PAWN SHOPS.**

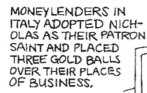

THE ONLY GEOGRAPHIC FEATURE IN TEXAS NAMED AFTER THE GENEROUS BISHOP IS ST. NICHOLAS LAKES IN NORTHERN REFUGIO COUNTY.

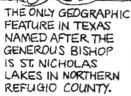

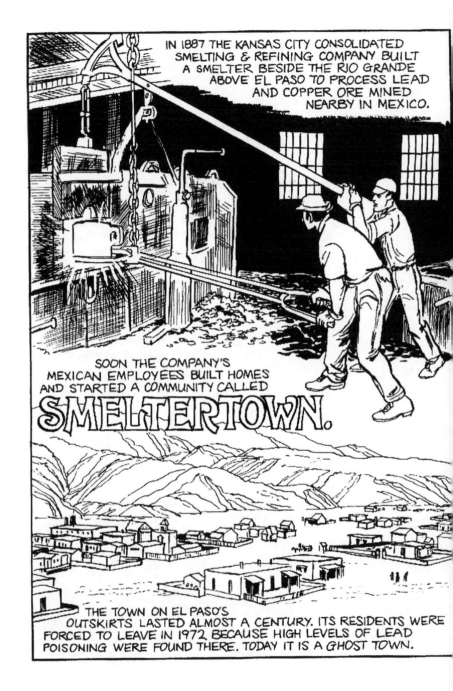

IN 1887 THE KANSAS CITY CONSOLIDATED SMELTING & REFINING COMPANY BUILT A SMELTER BESIDE THE RIO GRANDE ABOVE EL PASO TO PROCESS LEAD AND COPPER ORE MINED NEARBY IN MEXICO.

SOON THE COMPANY'S MEXICAN EMPLOYEES BUILT HOMES AND STARTED A COMMUNITY CALLED

SMELTERTOWN.

THE TOWN ON EL PASO'S OUTSKIRTS LASTED ALMOST A CENTURY. ITS RESIDENTS WERE FORCED TO LEAVE IN 1972 BECAUSE HIGH LEVELS OF LEAD POISONING WERE FOUND THERE. TODAY IT IS A GHOST TOWN.

Name Dropping

CANTON, A TOWN IN VAN ZANDT COUNTY, GOT ITS NAME FROM A HORSE RACE WHICH WAS WON BY A STEED NAMED *CANTER*. THE CITIZENS CHANGED THE LAST TWO LETTERS OF *CANTER* TO MAKE CANTON.

THE DISTANCE BETWEEN HARRISON COUNTY AND CADDO LAKE WAS THE SAME AS THAT BETWEEN ANCIENT KARNAK, EGYPT AND THE NILE RIVER, SO THE TEXANS CHRISTENED THEIRS **KARNACK.**

POST IN GARZA COUNTY WAS NAMED IN HONOR OF CEREAL KING CHARLES WILLIAM POST.

GOVERNOR ALONZO DE LEON LED AN EXPEDITION TO COLONIZE HIS PROVINCE OF TEJAS IN 1689. HIS SURVEYORS NAMED LANDMARKS AND DREW MAPS. WHEN THEY CROSSED A STREAM NEAR WHAT IS NOW SAN ANTONIO, SOMEONE EXCLAIMED,

HONDO!

THUS, THE SPANISH WORD FOR "DEEP" BECAME THE NAME OF THIS STREAM — HONDO CREEK.

IN 1881 THE GALVESTON, HOUSTON & SAN ANTONIO RAILROAD NEEDED A WATERING SPOT NEAR HONDO CREEK. THE COMPANY BUILT A DEPOT AND SET ASIDE LAND FOR A TOWN. THEY ALSO GAVE FREE RIDES TO ANYONE GOING THERE TO BUY PROPERTY.

THAT WAS THE BEGINNING OF THE MEDINA COUNTY SEAT, HONDO, TX.

A POPULAR SIGN

I.V. BELL AND **Z.O. BELL**, FIRST COUSINS, OPENED A STORE NEAR KILLEEN IN 1923. **JOHN HOOVER**, A LOCAL FARMER, ARTIST, HISTORIAN, AND SIGN PAINTER, OFFERED TO PAINT A SIGN FOR THE BUSINESS.

I'LL PAINT IT FOR **FREE** IF YOU LET ME DO IT **MY** WAY.

THE BELLS AGREED.

THE SIGN BECAME SO POPULAR THAT THE NEIGHBORHOOD'S RESIDENTS NAMED THEIR TINY COMMUNITY...

DING DONG

FROM SEAT TO SEAT

EARLY TEXAS LAW CALLED FOR THE BUILDING OF *FIRST CLASS* ROADS TO CONNECT **COUNTY** SEATS TO EACH OTHER. FOR EXAMPLE...

JACK	WISE	DENTON	COLLIN	HUNT	COOPER	HOP-KINS
JACKS-BORO	DECATUR	DENTON	McKINNEY	GREEN-VILLE		SULPHUR SPRINGS

AT FIRST THE ROADS WERE MERELY PATHS CLEARED TO A WIDTH OF FORTY FEET. IMPROVED TECHNOLOGY TRANSFORMED THESE ROADS INTO CONCRETE HIGHWAYS.

ALL ABLE-BODIED MEN, AGES 18 TO 45 WERE REQUIRED TO "VOLUNTEER" SEVERAL DAYS A YEAR FOR ROADWORK.

TREE STUMPS OF LESS THAN EIGHT INCHES IN DIAMETER IN THE ROADWAY WERE CUT FLUSH TO THE GROUND.

LARGE STUMPS WERE ROUNDED OFF SO THAT WAGON WHEELS COULD EASILY ROLL OVER THEM.

BOP!

BOSQUE COUNTY

KIMBALL
BEND PARK
MERIDIAN

CRANFILLS
GAP
CLIFTON
NORSE

TAKES ITS NAME FROM THE BOSQUE RIVER, WHICH RUNS THROUGH IT. THE RIVER WAS CHRISTENED BY THE MARQUIS de SAN MIGUEL de AGUAYO IN 1721 WHEN HE CAMPED ON ITS BANKS DURING ONE OF HIS EXPEDITIONS TO ESTABLISH MISSIONS IN EAST TEXAS.

SPARSELY INHABITED UNTIL IT BECAME A COUNTY IN 1854, BOSQUE COUNTY WAS SETTLED BY GROUPS OF IMMIGRANTS: THE ENGLISH AT PRESENT-DAY KIMBALL BEND PARK, GERMANS IN THE EASTERN PART, AND THE NORWEGIANS AT CRANFILLS GAP, CLIFTON, AND NORSE.

COMAL COUNTY

WAS CREATED IN 1846 BY THE TEXAS LEGISLATURE. *COMAL* IS A SPANISH WORD FOR "FLAT DISH" WHICH THE ISLANDS IN THIS PART OF THE GUADALUPE RIVER RESEMBLE. HOWEVER, COMAL COUNTY IS MOSTLY GERMAN.

Guadalupe River

CANYON LAKE

NEW BRAUN-FELS

SETTLEMENT IN THE COUNTY BEGAN IN 1844 WHEN A SOCIETY OF GERMAN NOBLES, MAINZER ADELSVEREIN, SPONSORED THE EMIGRATION OF 7,380 GERMANS TO TEXAS FROM 1844 TO 1847.

THIS WAS THE GERMAN LUTHERAN CHURCH IN NEW BRAUNFELS.

ON GOOD FRIDAY, MARCH 21, 1845, THEY FOUNDED NEW BRAUNFELS, THE COUNTY SEAT, WHICH THEY NAMED AFTER THEIR LEADER PRINCE CARL OF SOLMS-BRAUNFELS.

COMAL COUNTY'S FIRST NEWSPAPER WAS PRINTED IN GERMAN UNTIL THE END OF WORLD WAR II IN 1945.

Neu-Braunfelser Zeitung

DELTA COUNTY

IS NOWHERE NEAR A GEOGRAPHICAL DELTA. CREATED IN 1870 IT WAS SO NAMED BECAUSE IT RESEMBLED THE GREEK LETTER DELTA (Δ).

RATTAN
COOPER
N. SULPHUR RIVER
SOUTH SULPHUR RIVER

THE ORIGINAL RESIDENTS WERE CADDO INDIANS, A HIGHLY DEVELOPED SOCIETY OF FARMERS.

THE FIRST EUROPEAN VISITOR TO THE AREA WAS FRANCOIS HERVEY OF FRANCE IN 1750.

THE ISOLATION CAUSED BY THE RIVERS SURROUNDING THE PLACE MADE DELTA COUNTY A REFUGE FOR CRIMINALS IN THE EARLY 1800s.

THE FIRST PERMANENT ANGLO SETTLER WAS A MAN NAMED *BLUE* WHO BUILT A TRADING POST IN THE VICINITY OF RATTAN.

DIMMIT COUNTY

WAS NAMED IN HONOR OF PHILIP DIMMITT, ONE OF THE WRITERS OF THE FIRST DECLARATION OF INDEPENDENCE FOR TEXAS. HIS NAME WAS MISSPELLED WHEN THE COUNTY WAS CREATED IN 1850.

LEVI ENGLISH AND FIFTEEN FAMILIES FOUNDED THE FIRST PERMANENT SETTLEMENT, **CARRIZO SPRINGS** IN 1865.

WHEN DIMMIT COUNTY WAS ORGANIZED IN 1880, MR. ENGLISH DONATED LAND FOR A COURTHOUSE, SCHOOL, AND CHURCHES IN CARRIZO SPRINGS, THE COUNTY SEAT.

AFTER 1910, IRRIGATION AND A LONG GROWING SEASON MADE THE COUNTY ONE OF THE MOST PROLIFIC VEGETABLE GROWING AREAS IN THE COUNTRY. **ONIONS** ARE ITS MAIN CASH CROP.

FRIO COUNTY

WAS CREATED IN 1858 AND NAMED AFTER THE FRIO RIVER. *FRIO* IS SPANISH FOR COLD. THE ALARCON EXPEDITION TRAVERSED THE AREA IN 1718.

BIGFOOT ●
● FRIO TOWN
PEARSALL
◎
DIVOT ● DERBY ●
FRIO RIVER
DILLEY ●

RANCHING WAS ITS BIGGEST INDUSTRY. TILLMAN BERRY OWNED ONE OF THE FIRST SPREADS.

THE BUILDING OF THE INTERCONTINENTAL AND GREAT NORTHERN RAILROAD THROUGH THE COUNTY SPARKED ITS GROWTH IN 1881.

PEARSALL, NAMED AFTER THE RAILROAD'S PRESIDENT, THOMAS W. PEARSALL, WAS DESIGNATED THE COUNTY SEAT IN 1883.

THE OLDEST BUILDING IN PEARSALL, THE JAIL, IS NOW A MUSEUM.

HALE COUNTY

WAS CREATED IN 1876 AND NAMED AFTER LT. JOHN C. HALE WHO DIED IN 1836 LEADING COMPANY 7 OF THE 2nd TEXAS INFANTRY AT THE BATTLE OF SAN JACINTO.

PLAINVIEW
FURGUSON ●
● HALE CENTER
● ALLEY
ABERNATHY ●

THE FIRST SETTLER WAS HORATIO GRAVES, A METHODIST MINISTER WHO CAME WITH HIS FAMILY IN 1883. WITHIN TWO YEARS THE FAMILIES OF A.E. ADAMS, A.N. JONES, D.L. SHEPLEY, AND L.T. LESTER SETTLED NEAR WHAT WOULD BECOME HALE CENTER.

Z.T. MAXWELL AND E.L. LOWE FOUNDED THE COUNTY SEAT, PLAINVIEW, IN 1887. THE FIRST COURTHOUSE WAS INSIDE THIS BUILDING.

DRUG STORE

HARTLEY COUNTY

ON THE NEW MEXICO LINE WAS CREATED IN 1876 FROM BEXAR AND YOUNG TERRITORIES, AND NAMED FOR TWO LAWYER/BROTHERS— OLIVER AND RUFUS HARTLEY.

HARTLEY

CHANNING

ROMERO

THE COUNTY IS DEVOTED TO LARGE SCALE RANCHING. HEADQUARTERS OF THE XIT RANCH WAS LOCATED IN CHANNING.

CHANNING, THE COUNTY SEAT, WAS FOUNDED IN 1891 AND NAMED AFTER GEORGE CHANNING RIVERS, PAY- MASTER FOR THE FORT WORTH & DENVER RAILROAD.

CASIMIRO ROMERO CAME TO THE AREA IN 1876. HE OWNED 6,000 SHEEP.

LATER THAT YEAR, MR. ROMERO MADE A PACT WITH CHARLES GOODNIGHT THAT PREVENTED A WAR BETWEEN THE SHEEP AND CATTLE RANCHERS.

HE IS MEMORIALIZED IN THE COUNTY BY THE TOWN OF **ROMERO.**

LaSalle County

WAS CREATED ON FEBRUARY 1, 1858 AND NAMED IN HONOR OF RENE ROBERT CAVELIER, SIEUR de LA'SALLE.

LOCATED IN SOUTH TEXAS, NEITHER MEXICO NOR THE REPUBLIC OF TEXAS COULD CONTROL THE AREA. CONSEQUENTLY LASALLE COUNTY WAS A HAVEN FOR DESPERADOS AND HOSTILE INDIANS UNTIL THE 1850s.

JOSEPH COTULLA, A POLISH IMMIGRANT, ARRIVED IN THE COUNTY IN 1868 AND STARTED TO ESTABLISH THE REGION'S LARGEST INDUSTRY — CATTLE RANCHING.

MR. COTULLA SPARKED THE GROWTH OF LASALLE COUNTY BY DRILLING ARTESIAN WELLS AND ENTICING THE RAILROAD TO BUILD A DEPOT IN HIS TOWN, COTULLA, THE COUNTY SEAT.

GARDENDALE
COTULLA
ARTESIA WELLS
ATLEE

LIMESTONE COUNTY

WAS CREATED IN 1846. AT FIRST IT WAS HOME TO THE TAWAKONI AND WACO INDIANS. TEHUACANA WAS AN OLD INDIAN TOWN.

TEHUACANA
FORT PARKER
GROESBECK
KOSSE

THE COUNTY WAS PART OF THE EDWARDS-LEFTWICH EMPRESARIO GRANT. AMONG ITS FIRST SETTLERS WERE SILAS M. PARKER, MOSES HERRIN, LUTHER T.M. PLUMMER, AND SAM FROST. FORT PARKER WAS THE FIRST SETTLEMENT.

AFTER THE HOUSTON AND TEXAS CENTRAL RAILROAD WAS EXTENDED TO KOSSE, THE COUNTY SEAT WAS MOVED FROM SPRINGFIELD TO GROESBECK IN 1873.

MILAM COUNTY

WAS CREATED IN 1836 AND NAMED IN HONOR OF BENJAMIN RUSH MILAM, A VETERAN OF THE WAR OF 1812 AND THE LONG FILIBUSTER, AND A FALLEN HERO IN THE TEXAS REVOLUTION.

JONES PRAIRIE
CAMERON
GAUSE
NASHVILLE
THORNDALE

PRIMARILY AGRICULTURAL MILAM COUNTY ALSO PRODUCES OIL AND COAL.

CAMERON, THE COUNTY SEAT, WAS THE BOYHOOD HOME OF LAWRENCE SULLIVAN **"SUL" ROSS**, A CONFEDERATE GENERAL AND GOVERNOR OF TEXAS FROM 1887 TO 1891.

GEORGE CHILDRESS, ONE OF THE FOUNDERS OF NASHVILLE, TEXAS, CHAIRED THE COMMITTEE WHICH DRAFTED THE TEXAS DECLARATION OF INDEPENDENCE IN 1836.

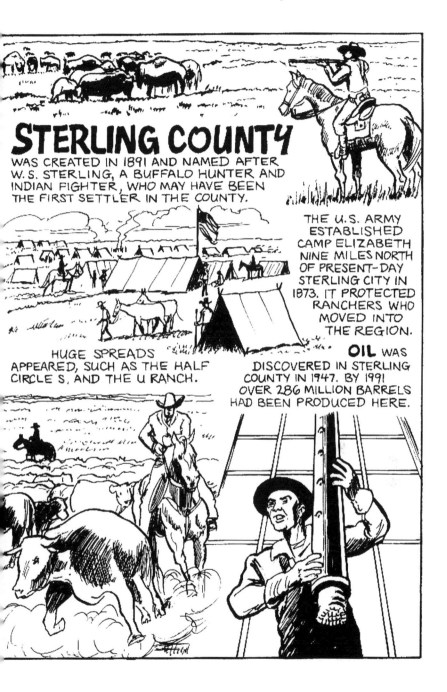

STERLING COUNTY

WAS CREATED IN 1891 AND NAMED AFTER W. S. STERLING, A BUFFALO HUNTER AND INDIAN FIGHTER, WHO MAY HAVE BEEN THE FIRST SETTLER IN THE COUNTY.

THE U.S. ARMY ESTABLISHED CAMP ELIZABETH NINE MILES NORTH OF PRESENT-DAY STERLING CITY IN 1873. IT PROTECTED RANCHERS WHO MOVED INTO THE REGION.

HUGE SPREADS APPEARED, SUCH AS THE HALF CIRCLE S, AND THE U RANCH.

OIL WAS DISCOVERED IN STERLING COUNTY IN 1947. BY 1991 OVER 286 MILLION BARRELS HAD BEEN PRODUCED HERE.

Part Five

The Big "D"

This rough map of the Dallas metropolitan area shows the location of the places mentioned in this section.

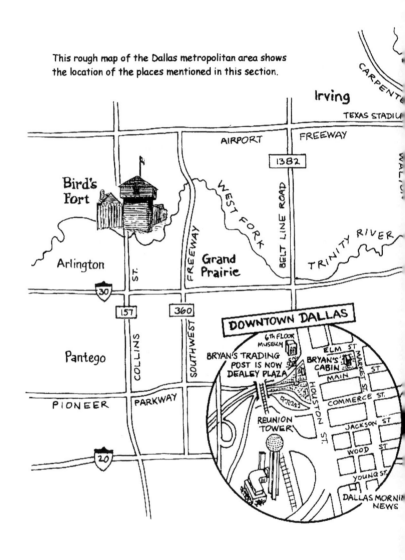

This Was Dallas

THE CADDO INDIANS ROAMED THE PLAINS OF NORTHEASTERN TEXAS A THOUSAND YEARS AGO. THE **ANADARKOS**, A CADDO CLAN, OCCUPIED THE AREA THAT IS NOW **DALLAS**.

THE FIRST EUROPEAN TO SET FOOT IN THE NEIGHBORHOOD WAS **LUIS MOSCOSO**, SECOND-IN-COMMAND TO HERNANDO DESOTO, DISCOVERER OF THE MISSISSIPPI RIVER.

AFTER DESOTO'S DEATH IN ARKANSAS IN 1541 MOSCOSO LED THE EXPEDITION OVERLAND TO MEXICO CITY. ALONG THE WAY THEY CUT ACROSS THE NORTHEAST CORNER OF PRESENT-DAY DALLAS COUNTY.

Early Visitors

SPANISH CONQUISTADORS PASSED THROUGH WHAT IS NOW **DALLAS** IN 1542.

NO STRANGERS VISITED THE AREA FOR THE NEXT 170 YEARS.

THEN, FRENCH TRADERS ANTOINE CROZAT AND BERNARD DE LA HARPE DID BUSINESS WITH THE ANADARKO INDIANS IN 1712 AND IN 1719.

IN 1760 FRIAR CALAHORRA Y SAENZ, A CATHOLIC MISSIONARY FROM NACOGDOCHES, PASSED THROUGH DALLAS MAKING TREATIES WITH THE INDIANS.

HE NAMED THE RIVER THAT RUNS ACROSS THE REGION THE TRINITY RIVER BECAUSE OF THE THREE FORKS WHICH MERGED TO FORM THE WATERWAY.

JOHN NEELY BRYAN WAS BORN IN 1810 IN TENNESSEE WHERE HE STUDIED LAW.

TO RECOVER FROM THE DEBILITATING EFFECTS OF CHOLERA HE MOVED TO ARKANSAS AND LIVED WITH INDIANS. EVENTUALLY MR. BRYAN BECAME A SUCCESSFUL LAWYER & BUSINESSMAN.

IN 1839 BRYAN AND A CHEROKEE COMPANION RODE INTO TEXAS WITH PLANS TO SET UP A TRADING POST ON THE TRINITY RIVER.

BRYAN ESTABLISHED THE TRADING POST THEN FOUNDED A TOWN AROUND IT WHICH IS NOW THE CITY OF DALLAS.

BRYAN'S BLUFF

AFTER SETTLING HIS ESTATE IN ARKANSAS, JOHN NEELY BRYAN CAME BACK TO A REMOTE SPOT IN NORTH TEXAS IN NOVEMBER, 1841.

ON AN 18-FT. BLUFF ABOVE THE TRINITY RIVER HE BUILT A CRUDE CABIN THAT SERVED AS HIS HOME AND TRADING POST.

THAT WAS THE BEGINNING OF **DALLAS** AND BRYAN'S BLUFF IS NOW **DEALEY PLAZA**.

It Was Almost Called Warwick

ON SEPTEMBER 4, 1839, WARREN ANGUS **FERRIS**, A SURVEYOR, RECEIVED A $5,000 BOND TO LAY OUT THE CITY OF **WARWICK** AT THE THREE FORKS ON THE TRINITY RIVER. UNFORTUNATELY, DROUGHT, SICKNESS, AND DESERTION RUINED HIS FIRST TWO ATTEMPTS.

FERRIS AND 29 MEN TRIED A THIRD TIME, BUT A DROUGHT DRIED UP THE THREE FORKS, MAKING IT DIFFICULT TO FIND THE STARTING POINT FOR THE SURVEY. MANY OF HIS MEN GOT SICK; OTHERS SIMPLY DESERTED.

FINALLY, FERRIS GAVE UP AND RETURNED HOME TO NACOGDOCHES.
A CITY NOW STANDS WHERE WARWICK WAS SUPPOSED TO... IT IS CALLED DALLAS.

THE GILBERT FAMILY

CAPTAIN MABEL GILBERT RAN A STEAMBOAT IN TENNESSEE WHEN HE MARRIED CHARITY MORRIS. THEY HAD ELEVEN CHILDREN.

IN 1837 THEY MOVED TO TEXAS AND WOUND UP AT BIRD'S FORT WHERE THEY MET J.N. BRYAN.

IN 1842 THE GILBERTS ACCEPTED BRYAN'S INVITATION TO JOIN HIS NEW SETTLEMENT ON THE TRINITY RIVER. CAPTAIN GILBERT BUILT TWO DUGOUTS IN WHICH HE MOVED HIS FAMILY FIFTY MILES DOWN THE WEST FORK TO BRYAN'S TOWN.

MRS. GILBERT IS IMPORTANT FOR TWO REASONS: SHE WAS THE FIRST ANGLO WOMAN TO SETTLE IN THE TOWN AND SHE CHOSE ITS NAME: **DALLAS.**

AFTER GOV. SILAS WRIGHT OF NEW YORK REFUSED TO RUN AS JAMES KNOX POLK'S VICE-PRESIDENT IN 1844, POLK SELECTED GEORGE MIFFLIN DALLAS, A PHILADELPHIA LAWYER. BOTH MEN ADVOCATED STATEHOOD FOR TEXAS, AND THEIR SLOGAN WAS

POLK, DALLAS, and TEXAS!

POLK WON THE ELECTION AND KEPT HIS PROMISE BY SIGNING THE BILL WHICH ADMITTED TEXAS INTO THE UNION ON DECEMBER 29, 1845. THE TEXAS STATE LEGISLATURE CREATED TWO COUNTIES ON MARCH 30, 1846 AND NAMED THEM IN HONOR OF THE PRESIDENT AND VICE-PRESIDENT.

DALLAS COUNTY ☐

POLK COUNTY ⟨⟩

JAMES KNOX POLK

GEORGE MIFFLIN DALLAS

The Old Preston Trail

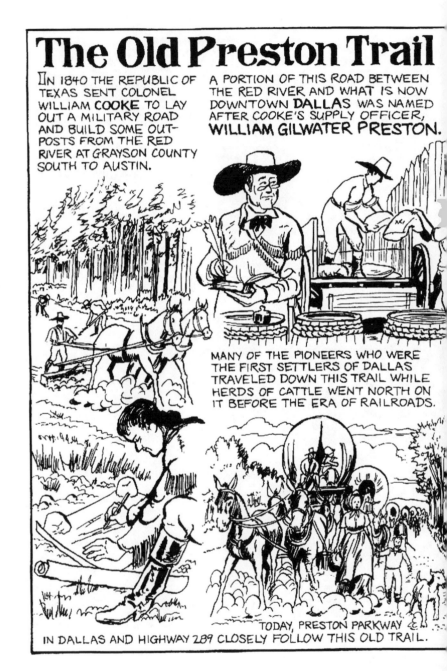

IN 1840 THE REPUBLIC OF TEXAS SENT COLONEL WILLIAM **COOKE** TO LAY OUT A MILITARY ROAD AND BUILD SOME OUTPOSTS FROM THE RED RIVER AT GRAYSON COUNTY SOUTH TO AUSTIN.

A PORTION OF THIS ROAD BETWEEN THE RED RIVER AND WHAT IS NOW DOWNTOWN **DALLAS** WAS NAMED AFTER COOKE'S SUPPLY OFFICER, **WILLIAM GILWATER PRESTON.**

MANY OF THE PIONEERS WHO WERE THE FIRST SETTLERS OF DALLAS TRAVELED DOWN THIS TRAIL WHILE HERDS OF CATTLE WENT NORTH ON IT BEFORE THE ERA OF RAILROADS.

TODAY, PRESTON PARKWAY IN DALLAS AND HIGHWAY 289 CLOSELY FOLLOW THIS OLD TRAIL.

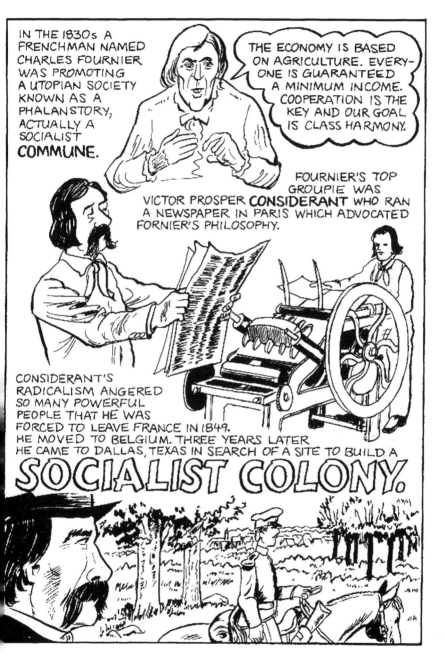

IN THE 1830s A FRENCHMAN NAMED CHARLES FOURNIER WAS PROMOTING A UTOPIAN SOCIETY KNOWN AS A PHALANSTORY, ACTUALLY A SOCIALIST **COMMUNE.**

THE ECONOMY IS BASED ON AGRICULTURE. EVERYONE IS GUARANTEED A MINIMUM INCOME. COOPERATION IS THE KEY AND OUR GOAL IS CLASS HARMONY.

FOURNIER'S TOP GROUPIE WAS VICTOR PROSPER **CONSIDERANT** WHO RAN A NEWSPAPER IN PARIS WHICH ADVOCATED FORNIER'S PHILOSOPHY.

CONSIDERANT'S RADICALISM ANGERED SO MANY POWERFUL PEOPLE THAT HE WAS FORCED TO LEAVE FRANCE IN 1849. HE MOVED TO BELGIUM. THREE YEARS LATER HE CAME TO DALLAS, TEXAS IN SEARCH OF A SITE TO BUILD A **SOCIALIST COLONY.**

IN 1852-53 A FRENCH SOCIALIST NAMED VICTOR **CONSIDERANT** TOURED NORTH AND CENTRAL TEXAS, GUIDED BY MAJOR HAMILTON W. MERRILL OF THE U.S. ARMY OUT OF FORT WORTH. ON THE WEST BANK OF THE TRINITY RIVER IN PRESENT-DAY **DALLAS** CONSIDERANT FOUND WHAT HE WAS LOOKING FOR...

A GREAT PLACE FOR A COLONY OF FRENCH IDEALISTS!

CONSIDERANT RETURNED TO PARIS AND WROTE A BOOK DESCRIBING HIS PLAN FOR A NETWORK OF SOCIALIST COMMUNES IN TEXAS. IT WAS TITLED

AU TEXAS.

THE BOOK WAS A HIT THROUGHOUT EUROPE.

AU TEXAS

PARIS, FRANCE— IN 1854 VICTOR CONSIDERANT (AT LEFT) ORGANIZED A COMPANY TO START A COLONY OF SOCIALISTS IN TEXAS. ITS CHIEF EXECUTIVE OFFICER WAS FRANCOIS JEAN **CANTAGREL.**

RECRUITING COLONISTS WAS NO PROBLEM, THANKS TO CONSIDERANT'S BEST-SELLING BOOK *AU TEXAS*. THOUSANDS OF EUROPEANS APPLIED TO BE COLONISTS BUT THE COMPANY SIGNED UP 200 FOR ITS FIRST SETTLEMENT IN TEXAS WHICH WOULD BE CALLED **LA REUNION.**

CANTAGREL PROMPTLY SAILED TO TEXAS AND PURCHASED 2,000 ACRES IN THE HEART OF PRESENT-DAY **DALLAS** AT $7 AN ACRE.

THE TRACT WAS ON A LIMESTONE SLOPE.

ZE LAND REMINDS ME OF FRANCE. WE CAN RAISE GRAPES HERE AND MAKE WINE TO SELL.

EARLY IN 1855 SOME 200 FRENCH, BELGIAN, AND SWISS IMMIGRANTS LANDED AT GALVESTON, THEN TREKKED OVERLAND TO NORTHERN TEXAS WHERE THEY STARTED A SOCIALIST COLONY NAMED

LA REUNION.

THE LEADER WAS VICTOR CONSIDERANT.

BY APRIL 1856 THIS UTOPIAN VILLAGE HAD A SOAP FACTORY, LAUNDRY, OFFICE BUILDING, A GROCERY STORE, A FORGE, A COTTAGE FOR THE EXECUTIVE AGENT, AND OTHER HOUSES.

IT WAS LOCATED WHERE THE FORT WORTH CUTOFF INTERSECTS WITH HAMPTON ROAD AND DAVIS STREET IN **DALLAS**.

The Last of La Reunion

BY 1860 THE FRENCH-SPEAKING SOCIALIST COLONY OF LA REUNION WAS DESERTED. THE LAST REMAINING HOUSE WAS OCCUPIED BY THE WIDOW OF ALFONSE DeLORD. SHE WENT BACK TO FRANCE IN 1861.

TODAY PART OF LA REUNION CONSISTS OF STEVENS PARK NEXT TO HAMPTON ROAD IN DALLAS. THIS MARKER COMMEMORATES THE OLD COLONY.

MANY DECEASED CITIZENS OF LA REUNION ARE BURIED IN THE OLD FISHTRAP CEMETERY, A HALF-MILE NORTH OF EAGLE ROAD IN DALLAS.

GUN MOLL BONNIE PARKER WAS BURIED HERE UNTIL HER CORPSE WAS MOVED TO CROWN HILL CEMETERY.

THE FIRST "STATE" FAIR

IN TEXAS WAS HELD IN **CORPUS CHRISTI** IN 1852.

IT WAS A THINLY DISGUISED LAND DEVELOPMENT SCHEME WITH TIES TO AN UPCOMING REVOLUTION IN MEXICO.

THE PUBLIC SOON CAUGHT ON TO THE RUSE AND STOPPED COMING. THE EVENT WAS A FLOP.

SEVEN YEARS WOULD PASS BEFORE ANOTHER FAIR WAS HELD IN TEXAS.

The First Genuine Texas State Fair

WAS HELD IN **DALLAS** IN 1859 NEAR A SITE THAT WOULD BE-
COME THE CENTRAL & PACIFIC RAIL YARDS. THIS FOUR-DAY
FESTIVAL DREW 2,000 VISITORS. EXHIBITS INCLUDED NEEDLE-
WORK, CARPETS, SHAWLS, QUILTS, PLOWS, VEGETABLES, FLOUR,
AND LIVESTOCK, ALONG WITH TESTS OF HORSEMANSHIP.

A SECOND EXPOSITION A YEAR LATER ATTRACTED 10,740 PEOPLE
OVER FIVE DAYS. BUT AGRICULTURAL FAIRS WERE SOON REPLACED
BY A MILITARY AFFAIR KNOWN AS THE CIVIL WAR.

STRIKES, SPARES, AND SINS

BOWLING WAS ONCE A RELIGIOUS RITE IN GERMANY.

PEOPLE CARRIED A *KEGEL*✱ OR STICK FOR PROTECTION DURING THE MIDDLE AGES.

THE *KEGEL*, WHICH SYMBOLIZED THE DEVIL, WAS SET UP IN A CLOISTER. BY ROLLING A STONE AND KNOCKING DOWN THE *KEGEL*, A PARISHIONER PROVED THAT HE OR SHE WAS LEADING A CLEAN LIFE.

✱THIS IS HOW THE TERM *KEGLER* CAME TO MEAN BOWLER.

GERMAN FRATERNAL GROUPS BROUGHT BOWLING TO TEXAS. PROBABLY THE FIRST INDOOR BOWLING ALLEY IN TEXAS WAS BUILT AROUND 1867 BY THE **DALLAS** TURN VEREIN. "TURN" MEANS *DO EXERCISES*; "VEREIN" MEANS *ASSOCIATION* OR *SOCIETY*.

The Bowling Champion

WILLIAM LILLARD WAS BORN IN 1927 IN FORT WORTH AND RAISED IN **DALLAS** WHERE HE ATTENDED WOODROW WILSON HIGH SCHOOL AND SOUTHERN METHODIST U.

AT THE AGE OF 23 HE BECAME A PROFESSIONAL BOWLER, THEN WENT ON TO WIN **SIX WORLD CHAMPIONSHIPS.**

BILL WON THE FIRST AMERICAN BOWLING CONGRESS (ABC) TOURNAMENT IN 1955. ON MARCH 24-25, 1956 HE WAS THE FIRST BOWLER TO TAKE FOUR TITLES IN ONE ABC TOURNAMENT.

A CHARTER MEMBER OF THE PROFESSIONAL BOWLERS ASSOCIATION, MR. LILLARD'S LIFETIME AVERAGE IS 207.

BILL IS A MEMBER OF SEVERAL HALLS OF FAME FOR SPORTS.

THE DALLAS TEXANS

SUFFERED FROM A CHRONIC LACK OF FANS. THIS PROFESSIONAL NATIONAL FOOTBALL LEAGUE TEAM PLAYED FOUR GAMES IN THEIR HOME STADIUM, THE COTTON BOWL, IN 1952 BUT THE COMBINED ATTENDANCE NEVER REACHED 50,000.

THE TEXANS WERE PLAGUED BY INADEQUATE PROMOTION, AN INEPT FRONT OFFICE, AND...

THE TEAM WAS STUCK WITH BAD PLAYERS LEFT OVER FROM THE N.Y. YANKS. THEIR ONLY WIN CAME IN THEIR LAST GAME, PLAYED IN AKRON OHIO, AGAINST THE CHICAGO BEARS ON THANKSGIVING DAY, 27–23.

TICKETS

YA WANNA TICKET ER WHAT?

ONLY 3,000 PEOPLE WATCHED.

TRY, TRY AGAIN

HALFWAY THROUGH THE 1952 SEASON THE NATIONAL FOOTBALL LEAGUE TOOK OVER THE OPERATION OF THE DALLAS TEXANS.

IN DECEMBER COMMISSIONER BERT BELL ANNOUNCED,

IF BALTIMORE COULD SELL 15,000 SEASON TICKETS IN ADVANCE, THEY CAN HAVE THE TEXANS' FRANCHISE.

IT TOOK A MONTH AND THE TEXANS BECAME THE BALTIMORE COLTS, NOW THE INDIANAPOLIS COLTS.

IN 1960 THE AMERICAN FOOTBALL LEAGUE LAUNCHED ANOTHER DALLAS TEXANS WHICH HAD A WINNING SEASON.

HOWEVER THEY LOST THE COMPETITION FOR FANS TO THE NEW NFL TEAM— THE **DALLAS COWBOYS.**

IN 1963 THE "NEW" TEXANS MOVED TO MISSOURI AND ARE NOW THE KANSAS CITY CHIEFS.

Part Six

Texas in the Early 20th Century

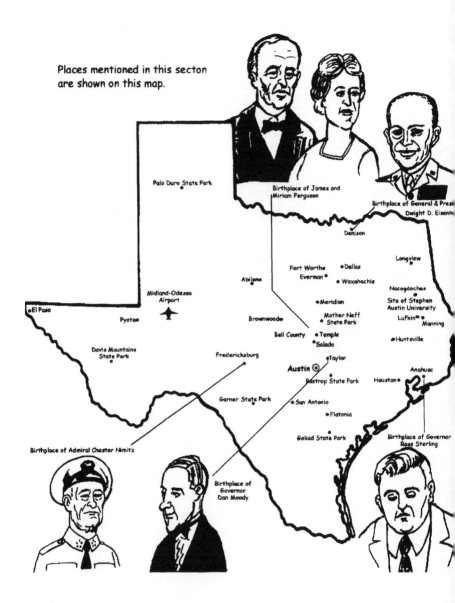

Places mentioned in this secton are shown on this map.

Palo Duro State Park

Birthplace of James and Miriam Ferguson

Birthplace of General & Presi Dwight D. Eisenh

Denison

Longview

Fort Worthe ● Dallas
Everman ● ● Waxahachie

Abilene

Nacogdoches
Site of Stephen Austin University

El Paso

Midland-Odessa Airport

Pyotee

Brownwoode

● Meridian

Mother Neff State Park

Lufkin● ●
Manning

Bell County

● Temple
● Salado

● Huntsville

Davis Mountains State Park

Fredericksburg

● Taylor

Austin ◎

Bastrop State Park

Houston ●

Anahuac

Garner State Park

● San Antonio

● Flatonia

Goliad State Park

Birthplace of Governor Ross Sterling

Birthplace of Admiral Chester Nimitz

Birthplace of Governor Dan Moody

BEFORE 1901 THE BIGGEST INDUSTRY IN TEXAS WAS

LUMBERING.

MOST OF THE TIMBERING OPERATIONS TOOK PLACE IN THE **PINEY WOODS** OF EAST TEXAS FROM BOWIE TO JEFFERSON AND HARRIS COUNTIES.

PEAK PRODUCTION OCCURRED IN 1907 WHEN TEXAS MILLS SAWED OVER TWO AND A QUARTER **BILLION BOARD FEET** OF LUMBER.

PRODUCTION EXCEEDED TWO BILLION FEET THREE MORE TIMES: 1909, 1913, AND 1916.

Manning-a Lumber Town

Lumbering was a major industry in Texas from 1880 to World War II. A big chip on the block was the Carter-Kelly Lumber Co. which, in 1903, erected a sawmill near the ruins of a mill built in 1863 by Dr. W. Manning. Annually the new mill cut 34 million board feet and employed 300.

A town named Manning grew around the mill in Angelina County. By 1900 it had 1,000 residents, two schools (one for whites and one for blacks), a post office, garage, movie theater, barber shop, drug store, and office buildings.

A RAILROAD WAS BUILT IN 1907 TO CONNECT THE LUMBER TOWN OF **MANNING** IN ANGELINA COUNTY TO THE COTTON BELT AND NEW ORLEANS RAILROADS AT HUNTINGTON. IT WAS THE SHREVEPORT, HOUSTON, AND GULF RAILROAD, POPULARLY KNOWN AS THE

SHOVE HARD AND GRUNT.

MANNING'S SAWMILL BURNED DOWN IN 1934 AND WAS NOT REBUILT. ITS CITIZENS MOVED AWAY TO LOOK FOR OTHER JOBS. THE HOUSES WERE REMOVED AND SOLD FOR THEIR LUMBER.

BY THE 1980s THE MANNING CEMETERY, TWO HOUSES, AND THE SAWMILL RUINS WERE ALL THAT REMAINED OF THE TOWN.

A Blacksmith's Biplane

BY THE SPRING OF 1912 JAN **PLISKA**, A CZECH BLACKSMITH IN FLATONIA, HAD CONSTRUCTED AN AIRPLANE—ONE OF THE FIRST BUILT IN TEXAS. JAN AND A FRIEND, GRAY COGGIN, HAULED THE PLANE TO A DRY LAKE BED NEAR MIDLAND FOR A TEST FLIGHT.

PLISKA IS SHOWN DRIVING THE WAGON... AND HIS AIRCRAFT.

HIS ENGINE FROM THE ROBERTS MOTOR COMPANY WAS TOO WEAK TO FLY THE PLANE VERY FAR.

PLISKA QUIT FLYING, THEN HUNG HIS AIRPLANE FROM THE RAFTERS OF HIS BLACKSMITH SHOP. IT REMAINED THERE UNTIL 1962 WHEN THE SHOP WAS TORN DOWN. HIS DESCENDANTS GAVE THE PLANE TO THE MIDLAND-ODESSA AIRPORT WHERE IT IS NOW ON DISPLAY.

TALIAFERRO FIELD WAS BUILT AT WHAT IS NOW OAK GROVE PARK IN EVERMAN, TARRANT COUNTY IN NOVEMBER 1917. AT FIRST IT WAS USED TO TRAIN CANADIAN FLIERS DURING WORLD WAR I.

AMERICAN UNITS STARTED USING IT IN APRIL 1918 AND RENAMED IT

BARRON FIELD

IN HONOR OF CADET ROBERT BARRON WHO WAS KILLED AT ANOTHER FLYING SCHOOL.

COVERING OVER 600 ACRES, BARRON FIELD HOUSED 150 OFFICERS AND 900 ENLISTED MEN. THE BARRON FIELD SENT SIX AIR SQUADRONS TO FRANCE BEFORE THE WAR ENDED ON NOVEMBER 11, 1918.

THE FACILITY WAS CLOSED IN 1921.

THE FLYING STINSONS WERE ORIGINALLY FROM MISSISSIPPI. BY 1910 BROTHERS EDDIE AND JACK WERE LICENSED PILOTS.

ENCOURAGED BY THEIR MOTHER (FAR LEFT) THE SISTERS TOOK FLYING LESSONS IN CHICAGO AND AT THE WRIGHT BROS. SCHOOL IN OHIO. ← KATHRYN BECAME THE COUNTRY'S FOURTH FEMALE LICENSED PILOT IN 1912.

TWO YEARS LATER HER SISTER, MARJORIE, AT THE AGE OF 20, BECAME THE YOUNGEST WOMAN PILOT OF HER TIME.

IN 1913 THE STINSONS MOVED TO SAN ANTONIO AND OPENED A FLYING SCHOOL.

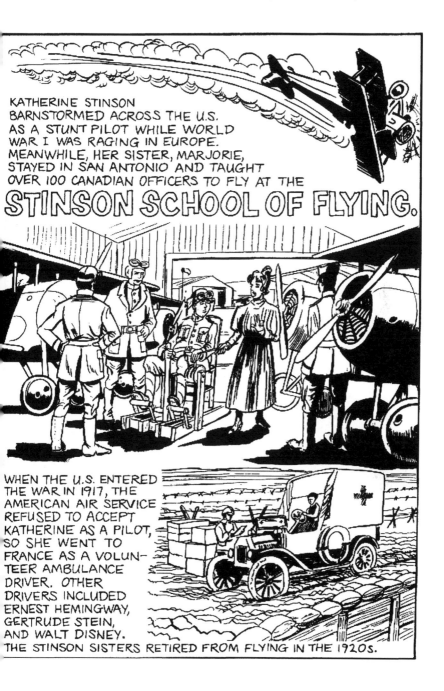

KATHERINE STINSON BARNSTORMED ACROSS THE U.S. AS A STUNT PILOT WHILE WORLD WAR I WAS RAGING IN EUROPE. MEANWHILE, HER SISTER, MARJORIE, STAYED IN SAN ANTONIO AND TAUGHT OVER 100 CANADIAN OFFICERS TO FLY AT THE STINSON SCHOOL OF FLYING.

WHEN THE U.S. ENTERED THE WAR IN 1917, THE AMERICAN AIR SERVICE REFUSED TO ACCEPT KATHERINE AS A PILOT, SO SHE WENT TO FRANCE AS A VOLUNTEER AMBULANCE DRIVER. OTHER DRIVERS INCLUDED ERNEST HEMINGWAY, GERTRUDE STEIN, AND WALT DISNEY. THE STINSON SISTERS RETIRED FROM FLYING IN THE 1920s.

PAVING THE WAY

THE FIRST CONCRETE HIGHWAY IN TEXAS WAS BUILT IN 1920 IN CAMERON COUNTY TO LINK HARLINGEN AND SAN BENITO.

THE FIRST FREEWAY IN TEXAS WAS COMPLETED IN 1951. IT CONSISTED OF SECTIONS OF THE GULF FREEWAY (IH-45) IN HOUSTON.

THIS SYSTEM WAS FOLLOWED BY THE INTERREGIONAL HIGHWAY IN AUSTIN AND THE DALLAS CENTRAL EXPRESSWAY.

"Pa" Ferguson's Good Works

GOVERNOR JAMES FERGUSON'S ADMINISTRATION GOT OFF TO A GOOD START IN 1915. CHAMPIONING EDUCATION HE CONVINCED THE STATE LEGISLATURE TO PASS A COMPULSORY EDUCATION LAW AND GIVE FINANCIAL AID TO RURAL SCHOOLS.

THREE NEW TEACHERS' COLLEGES WERE CREATED, ONE OF WHICH IS NOW STEPHEN AUSTIN UNIVERSITY.

CONSTRUCTION PROGRAMS FLOURISHED AS THE STATE PUT UP BUILDINGS FOR CHARITABLE INSTITUTIONS, COLLEGES, AND PRISONS.

The Verdict

THE TEXAS SENATE CONDUCTED A HIGH COURT OF IMPEACH-
MENT AGAINST GOVERNOR JAMES FERGUSON IN AUGUST 1917.
IN THE END THEY FOUND HIM...

AFTER HIS IMPEACHMENT,

IN 1917, EX-GOVERNOR JAMES FERGUSON AND HIS FAMILY WENT HOME TO **TEMPLE** IN MRS. FERGUSON'S "PRIDE AND JOY," A TWIN-SIX PACKARD. GOVERNOR JIM NEVER DROVE AN AUTOMOBILE. NEVERTHELESS, HE VOWED THAT ONE DAY HE WOULD RETURN TO THE GOVERNOR'S MANSION IN THE SAME CAR.

BACK IN TEMPLE THE FERGUSONS FOUND THAT MOST OF THEIR NEIGHBORS WERE NO LONGER FRIENDLY, SO THEY MOVED SIXTY MILES AWAY (TEMPORARILY) TO THEIR RANCH NEAR MERIDIAN IN BOSQUE COUNTY.

THE FERGUSONS ARE TOO HIGH AND MIGHTY IN THEIR BIG HOUSE AND FANCY CLOTHES.

THE FERGUSON HOUSE STANDS AT 518 N. 7th AT WEST FRENCH IN TEMPLE. IT IS CLOSED TO THE PUBLIC.

The Ferguson Ranch

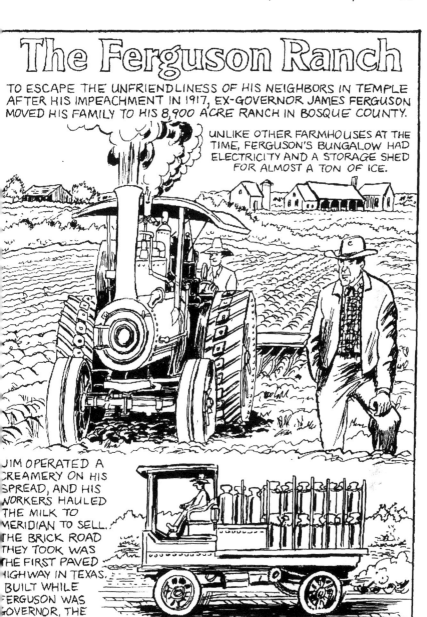

TO ESCAPE THE UNFRIENDLINESS OF HIS NEIGHBORS IN TEMPLE AFTER HIS IMPEACHMENT IN 1917, EX-GOVERNOR JAMES FERGUSON MOVED HIS FAMILY TO HIS 8,900 ACRE RANCH IN BOSQUE COUNTY.

UNLIKE OTHER FARMHOUSES AT THE TIME, FERGUSON'S BUNGALOW HAD ELECTRICITY AND A STORAGE SHED FOR ALMOST A TON OF ICE.

JIM OPERATED A CREAMERY ON HIS SPREAD, AND HIS WORKERS HAULED THE MILK TO MERIDIAN TO SELL. THE BRICK ROAD THEY TOOK WAS THE FIRST PAVED HIGHWAY IN TEXAS, BUILT WHILE FERGUSON WAS GOVERNOR. THE HIGHWAY EXTENDED SOME SIXTY MILES FROM HIS HOUSE IN TEMPLE TO HIS RANCH IN BOSQUE COUNTY.

The Slow Road to Recovery

REMOVED FROM THE GOVERNORSHIP BY IMPEACHMENT IN 1917, JAMES FERGUSON SOON WENT BROKE. ONE DAY HE WENT TO THE INSURANCE OFFICE IN AUSTIN OWNED BY HIS DAUGHTER, OUIDA, AND HER HUSBAND. NOT HAVING A CENT IN HIS POCKET HE ASKED HER FOR A LOAN.

HERE'S A CHECK, DAD, BUT IT MAY NOT BE GOOD BECAUSE WE DON'T HAVE MUCH MONEY.

HE NEVER CASHED THE CHECK BECAUSE A FRIEND GAVE HIM A LOAN. MR. FERGUSON STARTED A NEWSPAPER CALLED *THE FERGUSON FORUM.* HE HIRED HIS OTHER DAUGHTER, DORRACE.

I'LL WRITE MY OWN POINT OF VIEW SO NEVER AGAIN WILL ALL THE NEWSPAPERS OF TEXAS STOMP ON ME AND ME NOT ABLE TO SAY A WORD IN MY OWN DEFENSE.

Plan for a Comeback

GOVERNOR JAMES "PA" FERGUSON WAS IMPEACHED IN 1917, THROWN OUT OF OFFICE, AND BARRED FROM EVER HOLDING ELECTED OFFICE IN TEXAS. FOR THE NEXT SEVEN YEARS HE TRAVELED ALL OVER TEXAS SEEKING LOYAL FOLLOWERS WHO WOULD SUPPORT HIS POLITICAL COMEBACK.

SHOWN HERE— THE OLD GREGG COUNTY COURTHOUSE IN LONGVIEW.

THEN, ONE DAY IN 1924 AT A HOTEL IN TAYLOR, FERGUSON TOLD A REPORTER,

I PLAN TO RUN MY WIFE, MIRIAM, FOR GOVERNOR.

MIRIAM'S REACTION...

I ONLY FOUND OUT ABOUT JIM'S SCHEME WHEN I READ IT IN A NEWSPAPER.

The *GET EVEN* Candidate

IN 1924 EX-GOV. JAMES FERGUSON ANNOUNCED THAT HIS WIFE, MIRIAM, WILL RUN FOR **GOVERNOR** OF TEXAS.

AT FIRST I WAS ANGRY BECAUSE HE DID NOT INFORM ME BEFORE HIS ANNOUNCEMENT. THEN I DECIDED...

IT'S TIME TO GET EVEN WITH JIM'S "FRIENDS" WHO BETRAYED HIM, POLITICIANS WHO DOUBLE-CROSSED HIM, AND REPORTERS WHO RIDICULED HIM.

MIRIAM FERGUSON'S MAIN OPPONENT IN THE DEMOCRATIC PRIMARY HAD THE BACKING OF OVER 100,000 KU KLUX KLAN MEMBERS IN TEXAS.

ON THE CAMPAIGN TRAIL MIRIAM PROPOSED CUTS IN STATE SPENDING OPPOSED NEW LIQUOR LEGISLATION, AND CONDEMNED THE KU KLUX KLAN

☆ FELIX ☆ ROBERTSON FOR GOVERNOR

LET'S TRY TO LIVE UP TO OUR OWN RELIGION INSTEAD OF COMPLAINING ABOUT OUR NEIGHBOR'S RELIGION AND MAYBE WE'LL GET ALONG BETTER

MIRIAM AMANDA FERGUSON BEAT FELIX ROBERTSON IN THE 1924 DEMOCRATIC PRIMARY, THEN TROUNCED THE REPUBLICAN NOMINEE, GEORGE C. BUTTE, IN NOVEMBER. SHE WAS SWORN IN ON JANUARY 20, 1925, BECOMING THE

First Woman *Elected* Governor

IN THE UNITED STATES.

GOVERNOR FERGUSON ADDRESSES THE TEXAS HOUSE OF REPRESENTATIVES AT HER INAUGURATION.

MIRIAM AND HER HUSBAND, EX-GOVERNOR JIM, HAD SIDE-BY-SIDE DESKS IN THE EXECUTIVE OFFICE IN THE STATE CAPITOL. JIM DEALT WITH THE LEGISLATURE, BUDGET, CABINET OFFICERS, AND THE HIGHWAY COMMISSION.

MIRIAM DID EVERYTHING ELSE.

Pardon Me, Governor

INAUGURATED GOVERNOR IN 1925 MIRIAM "MA" FERGUSON MADE CONVICTS AND PRISON REFORM HIGH PRIORITIES OF HER ADMINISTRATION. SHE VISITED PRISON FARMS AND THE HUNTSVILLE PENITENTIARY TO INSPECT THE FACILITIES AND TALK TO THE INMATES.

WHEN WORD SPREAD ABOUT MA'S LIBERAL PAROLE POLICY, HUNDREDS OF PARENTS AND RELATIVES FLOCKED TO HER OFFICE TO PLEAD FOR THE RELEASE OF THEIR KINFOLK.

DURING HER FIRST TWENTY MONTHS IN OFFICE MIRIAM SIGNED 3,595 GRANTS OF EXECUTIVE CLEMENCY RANGING FROM FULL PARDON TO CONDITIONAL PARDONS.

PRISONERS WHO ARE NO LONGER DANGEROUS TO SOCIETY SHOULD BE PAROLED.

GOVERNOR ROSS SHAW STERLING REFERRED TO HIMSELF AS THE **FAT BOY.** IT WAS THE 265-POUND MILLIONAIRE'S GIMMICK TO ENDEAR HIMSELF TO THE AVERAGE CITIZEN.

UNFORTUNATELY THE COUNTRY WAS MIRED IN THE GREAT DEPRESSION DURING STERLING'S ADMINISTRATION, AND TEXAS HAD ITS SHARE OF MASS UNEMPLOYMENT, FACTORY SHUT-DOWNS, BREAD LINES AND SOUP KITCHENS.

WHEN THE "FAT BOY" RAN IN 1932 FOR REELECTION HE WAS DEFEATED BY NONE OTHER THAN...

FORMER GOVERNOR MIRIAM "MA" FERGUSON, HELPED BY HER HUSBAND, FORMER GOVERNOR JIM "PA" FERGUSON.

Farewell to the Fergusons

MIRIAM "MA" FERGUSON'S SECOND TERM AS GOVERNOR OF TEXAS ENDED IN 1935. SHE RAN ONCE MORE IN 1940 BUT LOST TO...

W. LEE "PAPPY" O'DANIEL.

IN ALL THE FERGUSONS TOOK PART IN 12 PRIMARIES AND FOUR GENERAL ELECTIONS AND WERE A FACTOR IN EVERY GUBERNATORIAL RACE BETWEEN 1914 AND 1944.

JIM "PA" FERGUSON SUFFERED A STROKE AND DIED SEVEN MONTHS LATER ON SEPTEMBER 21, 1944. HE WAS 73.

"MA" DIED OF HEART FAILURE ON JUNE 25, 1961 AT THE AGE OF 86.

THIS IS THE FERGUSONS' GRAVE IN THE TEXAS STATE CEMETERY IN AUSTIN.

FERGUSON

The CCC, CIVILIAN CONSERVATION CORPS, WAS A NEW DEAL PROGRAM STARTED BY PRESIDENT FRANKLIN DELANO ROOSEVELT IN 1933 AS A WAY OF PUTTING YOUNG MEN TO WORK DURING THE GREAT DEPRESSION.

MOST WORKED IN STATE AND NATIONAL PARKS.

MEN FROM THE AGE OF 18 TO 25 ENROLLED FOR SIX MONTHS WITH THE OPTION OF ANOTHER SIX MONTHS AFTER THAT. THE ARMY, AGRICULTURE, AND INTERIOR DEPARTMENTS RAN THE PROGRAM.

INSPECTION AT CAMP BULLIS NEAR SAN ANTONIO.

THE SOIL SOLDIERS

AT ITS PEAK AROUND 1940 THE CIVILIAN CONSERVATION CORPS (CCC) WAS EMPLOYING 19,200 MEN IN CAMPS ALL OVER TEXAS. MOST OF THEIR WORK WAS IN EROSION CONTROL AND SOIL CONSERVATION ON PUBLIC LANDS.

EACH MAN WAS PAID $30 A MONTH OF WHICH $25 WAS DEDUCTED AND SENT HOME TO HIS FAMILY.

The CCC and State Parks

FROM 1933 TO 1942 OVER 156,400 TEXANS WERE ENROLLED IN THE CIVILIAN CONSERVATION CORPS-CCC. THEIR LEGACY IS THEIR WORK IN THE TEXAS STATE PARK SYSTEM. THEY BUILT THIS TOWER IN MOTHER NEFF STATE PARK NEAR THE GROVE IN CORYELL COUNTY.

OF THE 56 STATE PARKS ESTABLISHED BY THE CCC IN TEXAS, 31 ARE STILL IN EXISTENCE INCLUDING BASTROP, DAVIS MOUNTAINS GARNER, GOLIAD, AND PALO DURO CANYON STATE PARKS.

They Were Not Just Work Camps

BETWEEN 1933 AND 1942 THERE WERE CIVILIAN CONSERVATION CORPS CAMPS ALL OVER TEXAS SUCH AS THIS ONE LOCATED A MILE WEST OF WAXAHACHIE.

THESE YOUNG MEN WORKED AT FORESTRY AND EROSION CONTROL. AFTER HOURS, THOUSANDS RECEIVED AN EDUCATION.

AT ANY ONE TIME ACROSS THE COUNTRY 20,000 MEN ATTENDED CLASSES FROM 5 TO 9, FOUR OR FIVE NIGHTS A WEEK. SHOWN HERE IS AN ENGLISH CLASS AT A CAMP NEAR LUFKIN.

SUMMER SOLDIERS

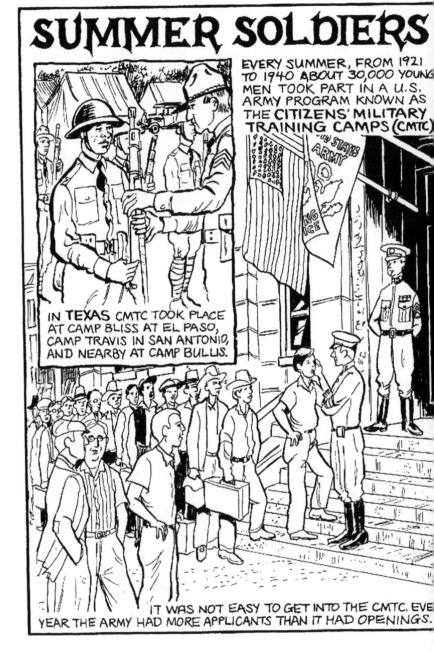

EVERY SUMMER, FROM 1921 TO 1940 ABOUT 30,000 YOUNG MEN TOOK PART IN A U.S. ARMY PROGRAM KNOWN AS THE **CITIZENS' MILITARY TRAINING CAMPS (CMTC)**

IN **TEXAS** CMTC TOOK PLACE AT CAMP BLISS AT EL PASO, CAMP TRAVIS IN SAN ANTONIO, AND NEARBY AT CAMP BULLIS.

IT WAS NOT EASY TO GET INTO THE CMTC. EVERY YEAR THE ARMY HAD MORE APPLICANTS THAN IT HAD OPENINGS.

The Rattlesnake Bomber Base

OFFICIALLY THE PYOTE AIR BASE, IN WARD COUNTY IN WEST TEXAS, IT GOT THIS NICKNAME BECAUSE OF THE PLETHORA OF REPTILES IN THE AREA.

ESTABLISHED IN 1942 ON 2,700 ACRES OF UNIVERSITY OF TEXAS LAND, PYOTE'S MISSION WAS TO TRAIN CREWS FOR B-25s (SHOWN ABOVE) AND B-29s.

AFTER WORLD WAR II IT WAS A STORAGE FACILITY.

S MANY AS 2,000 AIRCRAFT WERE STORED HERE INCLUDING THE *ENOLA GAY* WHICH DROPPED THE ATOMIC BOMB.

The Texans Who Ran the War

THE UNITED STATES FOUGHT WORLD WAR II ON TWO MAJOR FRONTS OR THEATERS, EUROPE AND THE PACIFIC, BOTH COMMANDED BY TEXANS.

GENERAL
DWIGHT D. EISENHOWER
WAS COMMANDER OF THE U.S. FORCES IN EUROPE (1942-43). IN JANUARY, 1944 HE WAS NAMED SUPREME COMMANDER ALLIED FORCES IN EUROPE. "IKE" WAS BORN IN **DENISON** IN 1890.

FLEET ADMIRAL
CHESTER W. NIMITZ
WAS COMMANDER OF THE PACIFIC FLEET AND HELPED PLAN THE "ISLAND HOPPING" STRATEGY THAT DEFEATED JAPAN. HE WAS BORN IN 1885 IN **FREDERICKSBURG**

Bibliography

Baker, D.W.C., comp. *A Texas Scrapbook*, New York: W.S. Barnes and Company, 1875

Baker, T. Lindsay, *Ghost Towns of Texas*, Norman, OK: University of Oklahoma Press, 1986

Corpus Christi Times, August 30, 1946, p. 2

Barr, Alwyn, *Black Texans—A History of African-Americans in Texas, 1528-1995*, Norman, OK: University of Oklahoma Press, 1996

Cohen, Stan, *The Tree Army—Pictorial History of the Civilian Conservation Corps, 1933-1942*, Missoula, MT, Pictorial Histories Publishing Co., 1980

Davis, J.T., *Legendary Texians, Volume III*, Austin, TX: Eakin Press, 1986

Dooley, Claude & Betty & the Texas Historical Commission, *Why Stop—A Guide to Texas Historical Roadside Markers*, Houston, TX: Gulf Publishing Co., 1985

Eisenhour, Virginia, *Galveston—A Different Place*, Galveston, TX Self-Published, 1983

Fehrenbach, T.R., *Lone Star—A History of Texans and the Texans*, New York: American Legacy Press, 1968

Flannery, J.B., *The Irish Texans*, San Antonio, TX: The University of Texas Institute of Texas Cultures, 1980

Haley, James, L., *Texas—An Album of History*, Garden City, NY: Doubleday, 1985

Hewitt, W. Phil, *The Czech-Texans*, San Antonio, TX: The University of Texas Institute of Texas Cultures, 1972

Holland, F.R., Jr., *America's Lighthouses—An Illustrated History*, New York, Dover Publications, 1972

Kington, Donald M., *Forgotten Summers—The Story of the Citizens' Military Training Camps, 1921-1940*, San Francisco, CA: Two Decades Publishing, 1995

Lich, Glen E., *The German Texans*, San Antonio, TX: The University of Texas Institute of Texas Cultures, 1996

McDonald, Archie P., *Nacogdoches—Wilderness Outpost to Modern City, 1779-1979*, Austin, TX: Eakin Press, 1980

McDonough, W., King, P, Zimmerman, P, comp, *The NFL Century—The Complete Story of the National Football League, 1920-2000*, New York, Smithmark, 1999

Miller, Ray, *Texas Forts—A History and Guide*, Houston, TX: Gulf Publishing Co., 1985

Moorhead, M.L., *The Presidio—Bastion of the Spanish Borderlands*, Norman, OK: University of Oklahoma Press, 1975

New Handbook of Texas, Austin: Texas State Historical Assoc. 1996

Newcomb, W.W., Jr., *The Indians of Texas—From Prehistoric to Modern Times*, Austin, TX: University of Texas Press, 1961

New York Times, Sept. 22, 1944; June 26, 1961

Paulissen, M.N. and McQueary, C., *Miriam—The Southern Belle Who Became the First Woman Governor of Texas*, Austin, TX: Eakin Press, 1995

Peterson, Robert, *Only the Ball Was White*, New York: Gramercy Books, 1970

Rickard, J.A., *Brief Biographies of Brave Texans*, Dallas, TX: Hendrick-Long Publishing Co., 1980

Sitton, T. & Conrad, J.H., *Nameless Towns*, Austin, TX: University of Texas Press, 1998

Stephens, A. Ray & Holmes, W.M., *Historical Atlas of Texas*, Norman, OK: University of Oklahoma Press, 1989

Stoff, Joshua, *Picture History of Early Aviation, 1903-1913*, New York, Dover Publications, 1996

Tarpley, Fred, *1001 Texas Place Names*, Austin, TX: University of Texas Press, 1980

Welch, J.R., *Building the Lone Star*, College Station, TX: Texas A & M University Press

_____ *Going Great in the Lone Star State*, Dallas, TX G.L.A. Press, 1976

Texas Sports Hall of Fame, *Its Members and Their Deeds*, Waco, TX: Texas Sports Hall of Fame

Tobin, J.L. and Dobard, R.G., *Hidden in Plain View—A Secret Story of Quilts and the Underground Railroad*, New York: Doubleday, 1999

Tyler, Ronnie, C., *The Big Bend—A History of the Last Texas Frontier*, Washington, DC: Department of the Interior, 1984

Writers Program, *The WPA Dallas Guide and History*, Washington, DC: The Works Progress Administration, 1936-1942

Index

A

Abilene, TX, 278, 306
Acapulco, Mexico, 25-26
Adams, A.E., 242
Adams, John Quincy, 54-55
Adams-Onis Treaty, 54-55
Adobe brick-making, 199
African-Americans, 67, 81,
    84-90; Negro baseball
    leagues, 195; State
    Senators, 211-212;
    Underground Railroad,
    207-209; James and Hiram
    Wilson, 210
Agriculture, 240, 246, 248, 270
Aguayo, Marquis de San Miguel
    de, 237
Ahumada, Colonel, 176
Alarcon expedition, 241
Alcalde, 115, 124, 146, 148
Alexander Hall & Co., 223
Alexandria, LA, 67, 69-70
All-American Girls Professional
    Baseball League, 196
Alley, TX, 242
Alpine, TX, 180, 213
Amarillo, TX, 180, 205, 224
American Football League, 275
American Air Service, 287
Anahuac, TX, 278
Andarko Indians, 252-253
Anderson family, 118
Andrews, Dr. Robert, 129-130
Angelina County, 280-281
Aransas Pass, TX, 180, 220

Arkansas, 123, 204, 252,
    254-255
Arlington, TX, 250, 256
Armstrong County, 225
Arnspiger, Harman, 192
Arrendondo, Joaquin de, 40-41,
    43, 104-105, 107-108
Arroyo Hondo Creek, 31
Artesia Wells, TX, 244
Atlee, TX, 244
Atomic Bomb, 319
Attorneys, 146, 188, 243, 254,
    261, 290
Au Texas (book), 264-265
Aury, Louis-Michel, 45-49
Austin, Emily, 99, 109
Austin, James, 99
Austin, John, 72, 78
Austin, Maria, 94-95, 99;
    marriage, 102
Austin, Moses, 75, 94-111; birth
    & marriage, 94; brother
    Stephen, 94; family, 95-96,
    in Missouri, 97-103, 109-111;
    lead business, 102-103;
    financial ruin, 102-103;
    struggle for empresario
    grant, 104-108; illness, 109;
    death, 111; statue, 111
Austin & Williams contract,
    168-171
Austin State Park, 144
Austin, Stephen F., 87, 92;
    birth, 99; education, 99-101;
    in business with father,

101-103; political office, 101; in Louisiana, 109-114; explores Texas, 113-115, 118; in Mexico City, 128-135; empresario grant approved, 135; founds San Felipe, 141-142; Fredonia Rebellion, 173, 176; named empresario, 144; founds Texas Rangers, 145; public education, 147; helps DeWitt, 152, 161; helps Robertson, 168; absorbs Leftwich's Grant, 168-169, 171; partnership with Williams, 169, 171; private life, 102, 148; Three Hundred, 87, 124, 137-138, 148

Austin, TX, 180, 215, 278, 289; baseball, 193-194; State Library, 219

Austin's colony, 116; capital, 141-142; German colonists, 163-165; government, 146; public education, 147; map, 149, 171; qualifications, 121-122; settler entitlements, 119, 125

Austria, 282

Aviation, 282-287; Barron Field, 284; Jan Pliska, 282-283; Pyote Air Base, 319; Stinson family, 285-287

Ayuntamiento, 146

B

Bacon Academy, 100-101

Bahia (La Bahia), 14, 17, 147, 150; Magee-Gutierrez expedition, 35-37, 61; Long expedition, 76-78, 82-83; Crossing, 124

Ballooning, 282

Baltimore Colts, 275

Banking, 185, 290

Barataria, 44

Barron Field, 284

Barrow, Clyde, 312

Bartering, 143

Baseball, 193-196; Negro League, 195; women's, 196

Bastrop State Park, 278

Bastrop, TX, 164

Bastrop, Baron Felipe Enrique Neri de, 105-107, 137, 141, 152

Bastrop County, 48, 153, 167, 171

Battles: Atlanta, 206; Chickamauga, 206; El Rosillo 37; Jenkin's Ferry, 204; Losoya, 40-41, 58; Molino Del Rey, 197; Murfreesboro 206; New Orleans, 44; Nolan's fort, 24; San Jacinto, 242; Shiloh, 206; Venadito, 48; Vicksburg, 206

Baylor University, 213

Bean, Peter Ellis, 26-28

Beaumont, TX, 180, 182

Beeman, John, 257

Belguim, Belgians, 189, 263, 266

Bell, Bert, 275

Bell County, 278, 290-291

Bell, J. H., 118; Z.O., 235

Belton, TX, 290

Bernardo Plantation, 139

Berramendi, J. M., 112

Berry, Tillman, 241

Bexar Territory, 243

Bexar, see San Antonio

Big Bend, 201-202

Bird, Major Jonathan, 256

Bird's Fort, 240, 256, 259

Blackburn, Ephriam, 25, 28

Blacksmith's Biplane, 283
Blanco, Governor Victor, 174
Blind, services for, 219
Bluebonnet, 226
Boarding houses, 88, 90, 164
Boerne, TX, 180, 190, 228
Bolivar Point, 65, 71, 81-85, 88
Bombers, 319
Bonham, TX, 180, 188
Bonnie Blue flag, 206
Bosque River, 237
Bosque County, 237; Ferguson's Ranch, 298-299
Bowie, James, 229; Rezin, 51
Bowling, 271-272
Boyden, Corp. John, 198
Brazoria County, 124
Brazoria, 88, 124
Brazos River, 29, 59, 61, 85-86, 114, 124, 126-127, 138, 149, 222
Brazos Indian Reservation, 213
Brazos County, 167, 171
Brewster County, 230
Brown County, 171
Brown, S. Leroy, 288
Brown, Maria (Mrs. Moses Austin), 94
Brown, Milton and Durwood, 192
Brownwood, TX, 278, 293
Bryan, James, 102
Bryan, John Neely, 254-255, 259
Bryan, TX, 180, 215-216
Buffalo, 205, 247
Burbank, Capt. Sidney, 198
Bureau, Allyre, 267
Burleson County, 171
Burnet County, 171
Burnet, TX, 180, 228
Burnet colony, 150
Butte, George C., 303

C

Cabazos, Jose Narcisco, 248
Caddo Lake, 2, 8, 180, 232
Cadets, 217
Caldwell County, 153
California, 92, 149, 286
Callahan County, 167
Calvit, Mrs. Alexander, 67, 70, 87
Cameron, TX, 246
Cameron County, 289
Cameron's colony, 150
Camino Real, 14, 29, 82-83
Camp Bliss, 318
Camp Bullis, 314
Camp Elizabeth, 247
Camp Travis, 318
Campeachy, 49, 53
Canada, Canadians, 287
Cantagrel, Francois Jean, 265
Canton, TX, 180, 233
Canyon Lake, TX, 238
Capote Baptist Church, 210
Capote Hills, 210
Carnegie Library, San Antonio, 219
Carondelet, Baron de, 22
Carrizo Springs, TX, 240
Carter-Kelly Lumber Co., 280
Cartoonist, 190
Cartwright Family, 118
Catholicism, 121, 253
Cattle, 201-202, 205, 241, 262
Caves and Caverns, 228-229
Cayuga (steamboat), 222
Cemeteries: Crown Hill, 251, 268; Fishtrap, 268; Manning, 281; Texas State, 313
Central & Pacific Railyards, 270
Channing, TX, 243
Charles County, MD, 66

Chatterjee, Dr. Sankar, 6
Cherokee Indians, 175, 254
Chicago, 285; Bears, 274
Chihuahua, Mexico, 25, 74, 92
Chihuahua Desert, 12
Childress, George, 246
Cholera, 162, 254
Christie, Capt. Lorenzo, 131
Christmas Creek, 230
Christmas Mountains, 230
Cigar business, 165
Circle S Ranch, 247
Citizens' Military Training
    Camps, 318
Citrus industry, 248
Civil Rights, 212
Civil War, 181, 197, 204, 206,
    211, 214-215, 220, 270
Civilian Conservation Corps,
    314-317
Claude, TX, 224
Clay, Senator Henry, 177
Coahuila y Texas, 149, 152, 154,
    159, 170; map, 92
Codes, 209
Cody, Buffalo Bill, 190
Coelophysis, 6
Coggin, Gray, 283
Coke, Governor Richard, 216
Colchester, CT, 100
Colleges & universities, 6;
    Baylor University, 213;
    Dartmouth, 73; land grant,
    216; Nursing schools, 218;
    Stephen F. Austin
    University, 278, 292; Sul
    Ross State, 213; Texas
    A&M, 215-217, 288; Texas
    Tech, 6; Transylvania
    University, 101; University
    of Texas, 191, 288,
    293-294; Wesleyan
    University, 214

Collin County, 236
Collins, Ted, 273
Colonization laws, 149
Colorado River, 14, 29, 34, 114,
    120, 125-127, 154, 157-158
Colorado County, 153
Comal County, 180, 238
Comanche Indians, 129-130,
    197-198, 213-214, 226
Commune, 263-268
Confederate States of America,
    197, 204-206, 214-215, 246
Connecticut, 94, 99-101
Considerant, Victor Prosper,
    263-266
Cooke, Colonel William, 262
Cooper, TX, 239
Copper, 232
Coral Snake, 227
Corps of Engineers, 8
Corpus Christi Bay, 181
Corpus Christi, TX, 180-181,
    269
Coryell County, 171, 316
Cotton, 139-140; first gin, 140
Cotton Bowl, 251, 274
Cotton Belt & New Orleans
    Railroad, 281
Cotulla, Joseph, 244
Cotulla, TX, 244
Country music, 192
Coushatta village, 59, 63
Cowboys, 187
Cranfills Gap, TX, 237
Crown Hill Cemetery, 251, 268
Crozat, Antoine, 253
Cypress Grove, 157-158
Czechs, 282-283

D

Dallas, Commodore Alexander,
    260

Dallas, Senator George Mifflin, 261
Dallas Cowboys, 275
Dallas County, 261
Dallas Texans, 273-275
Dallas, TX, 180, 250-276, 278; baseball, 193-194; Bird's Fort, 240, 256, 259; bowling, 270-271; Central Expressway, 289; first settlers, 252-259; football, 273-275 founding, 254-255, 257; French colonists, 263-266; La Reunion, 251, 266-268; map, 250-251; naming, 259-261; State Fair, 270; Texas Centennial, 312; utilities, 311-312
Davis Mountains State Park, 278
Dealey Plaza, 250, 255
Decatur, TX, 180, 236
Declaration of Independence, Texas, 240, 246
De Leon, Martin, 150, 155-161, 171
Delgado, Antonio, 38-39
DeLord, Alfonse, 268
Delta County, 180, 206, 239
Democratic Party, 291 ff; Convention, 312; Ku Klux Klan candidate, 302
Denison, TX, 278, 320
Denton County, 236
Denton, TX, 180, 236
DeSoto, Hernando, 252
Dewitt County, 153, 156
DeWitt, Green, 150, 152-154, 159; map of colony, 150, 153, 171; arrest and downfall, 160-163; Sara Seely, 153
Dice of Death, 25-26

Dickinson, J. B., 288
Dilley, TX, 41
Dimmit County, 180, 240
Dimmitt, Philip, 240
Ding Dong, TX, 180, 235
Dinosaurs, 3-6; Pytosaur, 4; Metoposaur, 5 Technosaurus Smalli, 6; Coelophysis, 6; Disney, Walt, 287
Distillery, 201
Drinking Fountains, 186
Dry goods business, 185
Durbin, Brazil, 154
Dyer, Leigh, 205

E
Earhart, Amelia, 286
East Bernard, TX, 185
Eastland County, 171
Economy, 143; Socialism, 263-268
Education: CCCs, 317; Flying School, 285-287; Public schools, 147, 291-292;
Edwards, Haden, 172-177; Benjamin, 172-177
Egypt, 233
Eisenhower, President & General Dwight David, 278, 320
El Paso, TX, 2, 10, 12-13, 17, 180, 188, 198, 203, 232, 278, 318
El Rosillo, TX, 37
Electric Companies, 311-312
Elguezabal, Juan de, 23
Elissa (ship), 223
Emperor Iturbide, 79-80, 128
Empresarios, 93-177; definition and qualifications, 93; map of grants, 150; see Stephen Austin, Burnet, Cameron, De Leon Martin, Green Dewitt, Haden Edwards, Filisola,

James Hewetson, Robert
Leftwich, James McGloin,
John McMullen, James
Power, Sterling C.
Robertson, Vehlein, Samuel
May Williams, Woodbury,
Lorenzo de Zavala
Enforcer, the, 32
England, English, 237
English family, 118, 240
Ennis, TX, 180, 226
Enola Gay bomber, 319
Ernst, Johann F., 163-165
Erosion Control, 317
Escambia, 160
Euless, TX, 257
Europe, 155, 287, 320
Everman, TX, 278, 284
Ewell, Capt. Richard, 199

F
Fairgrounds, Texas State, 251
Falls County, 170-171
Fat Boy, The, 309
Faver, Milton, 201-202
Fayette County, 153, 282-283
Ferguson, Dorrace and Ouida,
300
Ferguson, Governor James, 278;
290 ff; administration,
292-294; after his
impeachment, 298 ff;
announces wife's candidacy
for governor, 300; birth,
290; creates colleges, 292;
daughters, 300; death, 313;
education, 290-291; elected
governor, 291; elected
second term, 293; home,
298; indictment, 295;
impeachment, 296-298;
lawyer, 290; public
education, 291-292; ranch,
299; starts newspaper, 300;
University of Texas
squabble, 293-294; wife's
administration, 303
Ferguson, Governor Miriam,
278; 298, 300 ff; Bonnie &
Clyde, 312; Campaign, 302;
death, 313; defeated by
Moody, 305-306; defeated
by O'Daniel, 313; elected
first term, 303; elected
second term, 309-310;
electrifies Texas, 311-312;
hat gimmick, 310; Lower
Colorado River Authority,
311-312; pardons prisoners,
304-305; scandals, 305;
textbook contracts, 310
Ferries, 116
Ferris, Warren Angus, 258
Filibusters, 21-83, 104, 108; see
also Philip Nolan, Augustus
Magee, Samuel Kemper,
Bernardo Guiterrez, Dr.
James Long; trading posts,
59-63
Filisola's colony, 150
Firsts: Anglo baby born in
Texas, 85; Anglo colonists,
123; bowling alley (indoor),
271; commercial cave, 228;
concrete highway, 289;
cotton gin in TX, 140;
cowboy strike, 187; female
to fly the U.S. mail, 286;
freeway, 289; frontier fort
197; German colony, 163;
map of Texas in English, 22
millionaire governor, 308;
paved highway, 299; School
of Nursing, 218; State Fair
269-270; Texan at West
Point, 203; Texan of wealth

139; Thanksgiving Day, 11-13; theatrical performance, 13; U.S. Senators from TX, 184; woman governor, 303; woman to head a department in state government, 219

ischer, Alva Jo, 196

ishtrap Cemetery, 268

lags: Bonnie Blue, 206; Long's, 58, 73; Magee's green flag, 34

latboats, 182

latonia, TX, 180, 278, 282-283

loating Capitol, 222

loods, 117

lorida, 54-55, 219

lower, State, 22

ootball, 273-275

ordtran, Charles, 163

orestry, 317

ort Parker, TX, 245

ort Davis, TX, 203

ort Worth & Denver Railroad, 243

ort Cibolo, 180, 201-202

ort Worth, TX, 180, 192, 256-257, 264, 278; baseball, 194-195

ort Wayne, IN, 196

ort Bend County, 89-90

orts: Ben Franklin, 206; Bird's, 250, 256 259; Cibolo, 180, 201-202; Davis, 180, 203; Ewell, 180, 199-200; Inge, 180, 198; Jessup, LA, 64; Las Casas, 65, 81-85; McKavett, 180, 211; Old Stone, 58; Parker, 245; St. Louis, 15; Martin Scott, 180, 197

urnier, Charles, 263

France, French, 7, 15, 239, 253; in Dallas, 263-268; World War I, 284, 287

Franciscan Friars, 10

Fredericksburg, TX, 180, 197, 278, 320

Fredonia Rebellion, 172-177

Freeman, W. G., 200

Freemasons, 121

Frio County, 180, 241

Frio River, 14, 241

Frost, Sam, 245

Furguson, TX, 242

G

Gaines, Senator Matthew, 211-212

Galan, Jose, 147

Galveston, Houston & San Antonio Railroad, 234

Galveston, TX, 110, 150, 165, 180, 212, 222, 266; baseball, 193-194; Elissa, 223; Historical Foundation, 223; harbor and trolleys, 185; libraries, fountains, schools, 186, 218; haven for pirates, 45-51, 60, 62; Long expedition, 65, 68-76, 81-85

Garcia, Francisco, 77

Gardendale, TX, 244

Garner State Park, 278

Garza County, 2, 6, 233

Garza, Felipe de la, 141; Patricia, 155

Georgetown, TX, 180, 183, 228

Germany, Germans, 163-165, 237-238, 271

Gilbert, Captain Mabel, 257, 259; Charity Morris, 259-260

Glasscock, George Washington, 182-183
Glasscock County, 180
Goliad, 58; see Bahia
Goliad County, 153
Goliad State Park, 278
Gonzales County, 153-154
Gonzales, Rafael, 154
Gonzales, TX, 153-154, 161-162, 188
Goodnight, Charles, 205, 243
Government, Austin's, 146
Governors of the State of Texas: Richard Coke, 216; James Ferguson, 278, 290 ff; Miriam Ferguson, 278, 298, 301 ff; Dan Moody, 278, 305-307; W. Lee "Pappy" O'Daniel, 313; Sul Ross, 213-215, 246; Ross Sterling, 278, 307-309; youngest, 306
Governors of Texas under Spain: Alonzo de Leon, 234; Juan de Elguezabal, 23-24; Martinez, 75-78, 104-105, 112-113, 119, 128; Salcedo, 34-38; under Mexico: Victor Blanco, 174; Trespalacois, 86. 97-98; Felipe de la Garza, 141; Luciano Garcia, 144; Rafael Gonzales, 154
Grand Rapids, MI, 196
Grand Terre Island, 44
Grapes, 265
Graves, Horatio, 242
Great Depression, The, 309, 314-317
Great Britain, 55
Greenville, TX, 180, 236
Griffith, Corrine Mae, 191
Grimes County, 139-140

Groce, Jared Ellison, 138-140; Leonard, 140
Groesbeck, TX, 245
Grove, TX, 316
Guadalupe County, 153
Guadalupe River, 238
Gulf Freeway, 289
Gulf of Mexico, 46, 141, 149, 180, 207, 220, 260
Gunslinger, 188
Gutierrez, Bernardo, 20, 32-44 declares himself president of Texas, 38; Long's expedition, 56

H
Hale Center, TX, 242
Hale County, 180, 242
Hale, Lt. John C., 242
Hallettsville, TX, 153
Hamblen, William Henry, 224-225
Hamer, Capt. Frank, 312
Hardin, John Wesley, 188
Harlingen, TX, 289
Harpe, Bernard de la, 15, 253
Harris, William, 222
Harrisburg, PA, 222
Harrisburg, TX, see Houston, TX
Harrison County, 233
Harrison, William M., 117
Hartley County, 180, 243
Hartley, Oliver and Rufus, 243
Hartley, TX, 243
Hasinai-Caddoan Indians, 7
Hawkins, Joe, 110, 120
Hemingway, Ernest, 287
Herrera, Jose Manuel de, 45
Herrera, Gen. Simon, 30-31, 38
Herrin, Moses, 245
Hervey, Francois, 239
Hewetson, Dr. James, 150-151

Hill County, 171, 180, 191
Hinds, Geron, 154
Holtham, John, 146
Hondo, TX, 180, 234
Honeymoon Campaign, 306
Hoover, John, 235
Hopkins County, 236
Hospital-John Sealy, Galveston,
    218
Hotels: Ernst's Place, 164;
    Menger, 189
Houston County, 2, 7
Houston, East and West Texas
    Railway, 221; and Texas
    Central Railroad, 245
Houston Post-Dispatch, 308
Houston, Sam, 184, 217, 256;
    Temple, 217
Houston, TX, 163, 165, 180, 185,
    222, 278, 308; Baseball,
    193-194, 196; Democratic
    Convention, 312; Railroad,
    221; utilities, 311-312
Huling, Thomas, 182
Humble Oil Co., 308
Hunt County, 236
Huntington, TX, 281
Huntsville, TX, 180, 188, 278;
    Penitentiary, 304

Illinois, 182, 196, 274, 285
Immigration law, 162, 168
Impeachment: President
    Andrew Johnson, 212;
    Governor James Ferguson,
    296-298
Independents (ball team), 194
Indiana, 196, 275
Indianapolis Colts, 275
Indians, 7-9, 27, 108, 202, 239,
    244, 247; Andarkos,
    252-253; Comanche,

129-130, 197-198, 213-214,
    226; Cherokee, 175, 254;
    Fredonia Rebellion, 175;
    Hasinai-Caddoan, 7, 15,
    252-253; Jumano, 13;
    Karankawas, 81, 84-85, 124,
    136; Manso, 12-13;
    Nebedache, 7; Pueblo, 205;
    Seminole, 208; Tawakoni, 9,
    15, 245; Tonkawas,
    15;Wichita, 9, 15; Wacos,
    245; Magee-Gutierrez
    expedition, 33, 41; Long
    expedition, 59; territory,
    116; Trails, 224;
    Underground Railroad,
    207-208
Industry, TX, 165
Inge, Lt. Zebulon, 198
Ingram, Seth, 142
Intercontinental & Great
    Northern Railroad, 241
International Incident, 64
Interregional Highway, 289
Ireland, Irish, 16-17, 22, 121,
    151
Iturbide, Augustin de, 79-80,
    132-133; overthrown, 149

J
Jack County, 167, 171, 236
Jacksboro, TX, 180, 236
Jackson, Andrew, 27, 44, 54
Jackson County, 153, 156
Jackson, Humphrey, 146
Jalapa, Mexico, 27
Japan, 320
Jazz, 192
Jefferson, Thomas, 23, 30
Jenkin's Ferry, Battle of, 204
Jesuits, 10
Johnson, President Andrew, 212
Johnson County, 171

Johnston, James, 117
Jones, A.N., 242
Jones, Henry, 116
Jones, James W., 86; Randall, 86
Jonesborough, TX, 116-117
Joutel, Henri, 7
Jumano Indians, 13

K
Kansas City Chiefs, 275
Kansas City Consolidated Smelting & Refining Co., 232
Kansas-Nebraska Act, 184
Karankawa Indians, 81, 84-85, 124, 136
Karnack, TX, 180, 233
Karnes County, 153
Keenan, Tom, 257
Kemper, Samuel, 20-21, takes over from Magee, 36-39, 43
Kenny, Laurence R., 146
Kenosha, WI, 196
Kentucky, 22, 101, 182
Kerr, James, 153-154
Kiamata, 67, 81, 84-90; children, 90
Killeen, TX, 180, 235
Kimball Bend Park, 237
Kinney, Henry, 181
Ku Klux Klan, 302
Kuykendall, Abner, Joseph, and Robert, 123

L
La Bahia Crossing, 59
La Junta Presidio, 17
La Reunion, Dallas, 251, 263-266
La Sal Vieja, TX, 248
La Tablita, TX, 39
Lafitte, Jean, 44-45, 49-53, 62; Peter, 44, 49-53, 82

Lampass County, 171
Las Casas, 65, 70-71, 73-76
LaSalle, Rene Robert Cavelier Sieur de, 7, 244
LaSalle County, 180, 199-200, 244
Lavaca River, 160
Lavaca County, 153, 156
Lead Mining, 94-98
League, Hosea, 146
Lee County, 171
Leftwich, Robert, 166-168, 171, 245
Leftwich's Grant, 166-167, 171
Leon, Governor Alonzo de, 234
Lester, L.T., 242
Leverett, Sgt. William P., 198
Lexington, KY, 101
Libraries: Galveston, 186
Library of Congress, 219
Light Crust Doughboys, The, 192
Lighthouse, 219
Lillard, William, 271
Limestone County, 171, 180, 245
Lincoln, Abraham, 182
Lindbergh, Charles, 286
Lintot, Frances (Mrs. Philip Nolan), 23
Lively, 120, 125-127
Livingston, TX, 59
Lockhart, Byrd & James, 153
Loftin, Louis Santop, 195
Logistics: Long expedition, 72-73
Long, Ann, 66-69, 81, 84-89
Long, Jim, 90
Long, Dr. James, 20-21; brother's death, 61; children, 66-69, 81, 84-89; first filibuster expedition, 56-70; flag, 58, 73; raises army, 56-57; and Jean

Lafitte, 60, 62, 68-69, 82; Fort Las Casas, 65, 70-71, 73-76; logistics-2nd expedition, 72-73 marriage, 66; mutiny, 75; second expedition, 66 ff; 246; capture, 79; death, 80, 82; map and summary of expeditions, 82-83

ong, Jane, 66-71; 81, 84-90; marriage, 66; sister (Mrs. Alex. Calvit), 67, 70; at Fort Las Casas, 81, 84-85; widowed, 86-89; boarding houses, 88, 90; plantation, 89; death, 89

ong, Mary, 85-87

ongview, TX, 278, 300

oring, Lt. Col. William, 199

osoya, 40-41, 43, 58

ouisiana, 8, 14, 27, 44, 106 110-114, 119-120, 126-127, 150, 204, 211; Long expedition, 30-32, 41, 43-44, 49, 63-65, 67, 69-71, 83; French governor, 22; Railroads, 221

ouisiana Advertiser, 110

ouisiana Purchase, 30-31, 55

owe, E.L., 242

ower Colorado River Authority, 311-312

ubbock, TX, 2, 6, 180

ufkin, TX, 221, 278, 317

umbering, 279-281

utherans, 238

adison County, 34

agee, Augustus, 20-21, 32-37; death, 36

Magee-Gutierrez Expedition, 32-43, 58; summary and map, 42-43

Mahoney, Marie, 196

Mainzer Adelverein, 238

Malaria, 139, 141

Manchola, Rafael, 160

Manning, TX, 278, 280-281

Manning, Dr. W., 280

Manso Indians, 12-13

Map 234; of Texas in English, 22; Nolan expedition, 28, 29; Magee-Gutierrez expedition, 42-43; Austin's map, 114

Marfa, TX, 180, 201

Marlin, TX, 170

Marshall, TX, 180, 204

Martial Law, 308

Martinez, Governor, 75-78, 104-108, 112-113, 119, 128

Maryland, 66, 275

Massachusetts, 32, 310

Massacre at La Tablita, 39

Massanet, Fray, 7

Matagorda, 76, 82-83

Matamoros, Mexico, 149

Maxey, Bell, Senator & General, 206

Maxwell, Z.T., 242

McClellan County, 215

McCloskey, "Honest John," 194

McGloin, James, 150-151

McKinney, TX, 180, 236

McLennon County, 171

McMullen, John, 150-151

Medina County, 234

Medina River, 40-41, 43

Mediterranean Sea, 223

Menard County, 229

Menger Hotel, 189

Mercantile business, 182, 185, 235

Meridian, TX, 237, 278, 298-299
Merrill, Major Hamilton W., 264
Metoposaur, 5
Mexican Revolution, 10, 26-27, 269; aid from pirates, 45-49; insurgents take control, 74, 128
Mexican-American War, 197-199
Mexico City, Mexico, 79-80, 85, 86, 92, 128-135, 166, 252
Mexico, Mexicans, 14, 24, 27-28, 108, 128, 244; Army, 222; Copper, 232; map, 92; participants in Magee-Gutierrez expedition, 33; Long expedition, 74, 79, 82; Provincial Council, 108- 109; see also Republic of Mexico; Stephen Austin, 128-136; empresario, 155-161; Underground Railroad, 209
Mezieres, Athanase, 9
Midland, TX, 180, 278, 283
Milam, Benjamin Rush, 72, 78, 86, 246
Milam County, 171, 180, 246
Militia (Mexican colonial), 124; 145, 176
Millard, Henry, 182
Milling, 183
Millionaire governor, 308-309
Mills County, 171
Mina, Francisco Xavier, 46-48
Mina County, 48
Mining, 10, 156,
Mississippi, 23, 56, 65-67, 87, 219, 285
Mississippi River, 252
Missouri: 136, 153; Kansas City Chiefs, 275; Moses Austin's

settlement, 97-103, 108-109, 111; German colony 163; state legislature, 101
Molina del Rey, Mexico, 197
Monclova, Mexico, 14, 149, 162
Monroe, President James, 52
Monteauma, 11
Montero, Capt., 33
Monterrey, Mexico, 14, 85, 108, 130
Monuments: Moses Austin statue, 111; Texas Heroes Monument, 186; Drinking Fountains, 186
Moody, Governor Dan , 278, 305-307
Mooringsport, LA, 8
Morelos, Gen. Jose, 26
Morris, Charles H., 293
Morris, Charity, 259-260
Morton Cemetery, 89
Moscoso, Luis, 252
Mosquitos, 200
Mother Neff State Park, 316
Mother of Texas, see Long, Jane
Motion Pictures, 191
Mound Prairie, 27
Muldoon, Father Michael, 121
Museum of Southern History, 89
Music, 192
Musick, James, 154
Muskegon, MI, 196
Musquiz, Lt., 24
Mustanging, 22, 24
Mutiny, 75

N
Nacogdoches, TX, 24, 27, 150, 180, 253, 258, 278; Fredonia Rebellion, 172-17 Long expedition, 57-58,

62-64; Magee-Gutierrez
expedition, 33-34; Nolan's
expedition, 57-58, 68,
82-83; Stephen Austin, 118,
149; Railroads, 221
Nahsville Company, 168-169
Nashville, TN, 166-169
Nashville, TX, 246
Natchez, MS, 23, 56-57, 65-67,
87
Natchitoches, LA, 14, 110-112
National Football League,
273-275
National Parks, 314
Navarro, Jose, 153
Nebedache Indians, 7
Negro baseball leagues, 195
Neutral Ground, 31-32
New York, 163, 218, 261, 273
New Mexico, 11-12, 92, 149,
203, 205
New Deal, 314
New Orleans, LA, 27, 103, 110,
120, 126-127; Battle of, 44
New Braunfels, 228, 238
New York Yanks, 273-274
New Orleans, LA, 27, 103, 110,
193; Battle of, 44; German
colonists, 163
New Spain, 14, 16-17;
Adams-Onis Treaty, 55-56;
dealing with colonists,
104-108, 156; dealing with
filibusters, 30 ff, 108;
education, 147; leadership,
104; viceroy, 104
Newspapers, 301; Criticize
Governor James Ferguson,
293; Houston Post-Dispatch,
308; San Antonio Express,
190; Baltimore Sun, 177;
Ferguson Forum, 300; New

Braunfelser Zielung, 238;
socialist, 263
Nimitz, Admiral Chester W.,
278, 320
Ninth Infantry Regiment of
Texas, 206
Nolan County, 24
Nolan, Philip, 20, 22-26, 58;
makes first map of Texas in
English, 22; death, 24;
summary of mission, 28-29
Norse, TX, 237
Norway, Norwegians, 237
Nueces River, 14, 29, 149-150,
199-200
Nursing, 218

O
O'Connor, Hugh, 16-17
O'Daniel, Governor W. Lee
"Pappy," 313
O'Rielly, James, 151
O'Toole, 151
Odessa, TX, 180, 278, 283
Ohio, 274, 285
Oil production, 246-247, 308
Oklahoma, 9, 116
Old Stone Fort, 58
Old Station port, 160
Onate, Juan de, 11-13
Onions, 240, 248
Onis, Louis de, 55
Orchid of the Silver Screen,
191
Oregon Territory, 55, 92
Orphanages, 186
Outlaws, 188, 244

P
Palestine, TX, 2, 9, 27
Palo Duro Canyon, 180, 224-225
Palo Pinto County, 171
Palo Duro State Park, 278

Pangea, 3
Panhandle, 3-4, 187, 205
Paris, France, 264
Parker, Bonnie, 268, 312
Parker, Silas M., 245
Parker, Cynthia Ann, 214
Parker County, 171
Parole policy, 304-305, 307
Pawn Shops, 231
Paxton, Mildred, 306
Pearsall, TX, 241
Pearsall, Thomas W., 241
Pecan Point, TX, 59
Pennsylvania, 94, 195, 218, 222,
    260-261
Peoria, IL, 196
Perez, Col. Ignacio, 61-63, 78,
    82
Perry, Henry, 40-41
Philadelphia, PA, 94, 195, 218,
    260-261
Phytosaur, 4
Piney Woods, 221, 279
Pirates, 24-25, 44-53, 260; see
    also Jean Lafitte,
    Louis-Michel Aury
Plainview, TX, 242
Plantations, 139-140
Pliska, Jan, 282-283
Plummer, Luther T.M., 245
Poland, Polish, 244
Politics, elections, 215
Polk County, 63, 261
Post, Charles William, 233
Polk, President James Knox, 261
Post quarry, 6
Post, TX, 180, 233
Potosi, MO, 98, 102, 108-109
Pottery making, 210
Powell's Cave, 180, 229
Power Dams, 311-312
Power, James, 150-151

Presidents of the Republic of
    Texas: David G. Burnet,
    222, Sam Houston, 256
Presidents of the U. S.: John
    Quincy Adams, 54-55;
    Dwight D. Eisenhower, 278,
    320; Andrew Jackson, 27,
    44, 54; Thomas Jefferson,
    23, 30; Andrew Johnson,
    212; Abraham Lincoln, 182;
    James Monroe, 52, 54;
    James Knox Polk, 261;
    Franklin Delano Roosevelt,
    314; Theodore Roosevelt,
    189
Presidios, 16-17
Preston, Isaac T., 72
Preston Road, 251, 262
Preston, William Gilwater, 262
Prisons, 25, 188, 292, 304, 307
Protestantism, 121
Provincial Council of Mexico,
    108-109, 168, 170
Pueblo Indians, 205
Pyote, TX, 278, 319

Q
Quiltmaking, 209

R
"Rabbit, The," 221
R.E. Lees (ball team), 193
Racine, WI, 196
Radio, 192, 288
Railroads, 184-185, 221,
    224-226, 234, 241, 243,
    245, 270, 281, 308; first
    paved highway in Texas,
    299; State Highway Dept.
    created, 293
Ramon, Domingo, 7

anches, Ranching, 201-202,
205, 241-244, 247; XIT,
243
andal, Horace, 203-205
andall County, 180, 205
attan, TX, 239
attlesnake Bomber Base, 319
econstruction, 211-212
ed River, 8, 14, 59, 67,
116-117, 149, 221
efugio County, 231
efugio, TX, 150-151
egidores, 146, 148
epublic of Fredonia, 175-177
epublic of Texas, 88, 181, 244,
256; Nolan's, 34; Long's, 57
ff; Capitol, 222; Congress,
117; roads, 262
epublic of Mexico, 93-177,
163; Austin reapplies for
grant, 130-135; Congress,
132, 135; grants empresario
title to Austin, to DeWitt,
152, to DeLeon, 157, to
Nashville Co./Leftwich, 166;
immigration law, 162, 168;
Fredonia Rebellion, 172-177;
Lafitte's government, 50-51;
map, 92, 144; presidents,
158
epublican Army of the North,
33-43
epublican Party, 303
chmond, TX, 88-89
ver, Thad W., 117
Grande, 13-14, 29, 149, 208,
232
oley, Gen. Eleazer Wheelock,
72-74
vers, George Channing, 243
ads and highways, 14,
197-199, 236, 262, 289;
first paved highway, 299

Roberts Motor Company, 283
Robertson, Felix, 303
Robertson County, 171, 211
Robertson, Sterling Clack,
168-171; Sarah, 170
Robertson's Colony, 150, 169-171
Robinson, Andrew, 123-124;
Nancy, 123
Rockford, IL, 196
Rome, Italy, 51
Romero, TX, 243
Romero, Casimiro, 243
Roosevelt, Theodore, 189
Rosenberg, Henry, 185-186
Rosenberg, TX, 180, 185
Ross, Governor & Gen. Lawrence
Sullivan, 213-215, 246
Ruby, Senator George
Thompson, 212
Rusk, Senator Thomas J., 184

S
Sabine River, 29, 31, 63-64,
107, 221
Saenz, Friar Calahorra y, 253
Salado, TX, 278, 290
Salcedo, Governor, 34-38
Saltillo, Mexico, 14, 92, 152, 168
San Felipe de Austin, 92,
141-142, 145, 150, 163-165,
180, 222
San Francisco de los Tejas
mission, 7
San Augustine, TX, 180, 203
San Antonio River, 29, 114
San Antonio, TX, 14, 17, 28, 33,
34, 41, 62, 92, 150, 189,
234, 278; Moses Austin,
104-109, 111; Stephen
Austin, 113-115, 128-130,
141, 147, 149; baseball, 194,
196; captured by Magee's
army, 33, 37-39; Carnegie

Library, 219; CCC camps, 314; CMTC camps, 318; Express, 190; filibusters imprisoned, 25, 79; Long expedition, 75, 82, 86-87; roads and forts, 197-199; Rough Riders, 189; Stinsons, 285-287
San Benito, 289
San Jacinto: Battle, 242; Day, 193
San Marcos River, 154
San Marcos, TX, 228
Santa Anna, 222
Santa Gertrudis de Altar Presidio, 17
Santa Fe Railroad, 185
Santa Rosa Presidio, 17
Santop, Louis "Top," 195
Sarahville de Viesca, TX, 170
Saucedo-political chief, 161
Scott, Lt. Col. Martin, 197
Sealy, John, 218
Seguin, Don Erasmo, 112, 115
Seguin, TX, 153, 180, 210
Seminole Indians, 208; War, 54
Senators, U.S., 184
Sheep ranching, 243
Shepley, D.L., 242
Ships: Lively, 120, 125-127; Elissa, 223; Escambia, 160
Shove Hard and Grunt Railroad, 281
Shreveport, Houston, and Gulf Railroad, 281
Signs, 235
Silver, 10, 229
Silverton, TX, 180, 224
Simonson, Major J. S., 200
Slaves, slavery: 139-140, 184; Austin's, 96; Trading, 51; Underground Railroad, 207-209

Smeltertown, TX, 180, 232
Smith, Erastus "Deaf," 154
Smugglers & smuggling, 31, 44, 160-161, 181, 223
Snakes, 227, 319
Socialism, 263-268
Solms-Braunfels, Prince Carl, 238
Somerville County, 171
Sonora y Sinaloa, 92
Sonora, TX, 228
Spain, Spanish, 9-14, 16-17, 79, 97-98, 219, 238, 241, 248; Dallas, 253-254; roads, 14, see also Filibusters, Mexican Revolution, New Spain
Spanish-American War, 189
Spanish Main, 51
Springfield IL, 182, 196
Springfield, TX, 245
St. Genevieve, MO, 97
St. Louis, MO, 96-98
St. Nicholas, 231
St. Nicholas Lakes, 180, 231
St. Philip de Bethsaida, 141
State Senators, 211-212
State Parks, 314, 316; Austin, 144; Bastrop, 278, 316; Davis Mountains, 278, 316; Garner State Park, 278, 316; Goliad, 278, 316; Mother Neff, 278, 316; Pal Duro, 278, 316
State Librarian, 219
State Fair, 269-270
Statehood, 261
Steamboats, 117, 182, 259; floating capitol, 222
Stein, Gertrude, 287
Stephen Austin University, 278 292

terling County, 171, 180, 182, 247
terling, Governor Ross Shaw, 278, 307-309
terling, W.S., 247
tevens Park, Dallas, 251, 268
tinson, Eddie, 285; Jack, 285; Kathryn, 285-287; Marjorie, 285, 287
tonewalls of Houston, 193
trickland, Mr. (No first name), 154
trikes, 187
ullivan, James S., 89
ulphur River, 239
ulphur Springs, 180, 236
ummer Soldiers, 318
urveyors, 142, 154, 163, 258
witzerland, Swiss, 185-186, 266

aliaferro Field, 284
amaulipas, Mex, 155
arrant County, 171
ascosa, TX, 180, 187
awakoni Indians, 9, 245
aylor, Nannie, 204
aylor, TX, 278, 300
echnosaurus Smalli, 6
ehuacana, TX, 245
emple, TX, 278, 298-299
enant Farmers' Rent Control Law, 291
ennessee, 166-169, 254, 259
exarkana, TX, 2, 15
exas A & M University, 215-217, 288
exas Association, 166-168
exas Centennial Commission, 111
exas Free Library, 219
exas Heroes Monument, 186

Texas Highway Department, 293; Commission, 305, 307
Texas League (baseball), 194
Texas Rangers, 145, 213-214, 256, 312
Texas Revolution, 222, 242, 246
Texas State Cemetery, 313
Texas State Legislature, 184, 226, 238, 248, 261, 296, 312
Texas State Senate, 211-212, 297
Texas Tech University, 6
Thanksgiving Day, 11-13, 274
Theatrical performance, first, 13
Thomson, Alex, 168
Three Hundred, Austin's, 87, 124, 137-138, 148
Tinsley, Lizzie, 214
Tobacco Business, 165; Incident, 160
Toepperwein, Adolph "Ad," 190
Toledo, Alvarez de, 39-41, 43
Trading Posts: Bryan's, 254-255; Filibuster, 59-61, 82-83
Transcontinental Railroad, 184
Transylvania University, 101
Travis County, 295
Trespalacois, Jose Felix, 74-77, 86
Triassic period, 3-6
Trinidad de Salcedo (Spanish villa), 34
Trinity River, 14, 29, 34, 59, 62, Dallas, 250-251, 253-255, 257-259, 264
Trolley lines, 185
Tyler, TX, 180, 195

U

Underground Railroad, 207-209

United States, 126, 161; Capitol,
184; Conspires to overthrow
Spanish in Mexico, 23, 47;
Dept. of Agriculture, 314;
Dept. of Interior, 314;
Fredonia Rebellion, 173-174,
177; government, 116, 184;
Mail, 286; Senators, 184;
ships attacked by pirates,
52
United States Army, 72,
197-201, 203-204, 247,
264; administers CCC, 314;
CMTC, 318
United States Navy, 52-53,
260, 320
Universities: see Colleges &
Universities
University of Texas, 191, 288,
319; fight with Governor
James Ferguson, 293-294,
296
Utilities, 311
Uvalde County, 198

V

Van Zandt County, 233
Vehlein, colony, 150
Velasco, TX, 222
Venadito, Mexico, 48
Viceroy, 11; Apodaca, 104
Victoria County, 153, 156, 158
Victoria, Guadalupe, 158
Victoria, TX, 153, 158-159
Vidor, King, 191
Viesca, Augustin, 170
Virginia, 94-96

W

Waco, TX, 2, 9, 24-25, 58, 180,
193, 213, 230; Indians, 245
Waller County, 124, 139-140
War of 1812, 44, 73, 260

Ward County, 319
Wars: Seminole, 54; War of
1812, 44, 73, 260; Civil, 181,
197, 204, 206, 211, 214-215,
220, 270;
Mexican-American, 197-199
Spanish-American, 189;
World War I, 284, 287;
World War II, 196, 238,
280, 319-320
Warwick (Dallas), 258
Washington County, TX, 124,
211-212
Washington, TX, 59, 124, 180
Waters, (no first name),
129-130
Waxahachie, TX, 278, 317
Wayside, TX, 224
Webb, Isaac B., 257
Weltens, Edward, 189
Wesleyan University, 214
West, Elizabeth Howard, 218
West Point, NY (U.S. Military
Academy), 32, 203
Western Pygmy Rattlesnakes,
227
Western Swing music, 192
Whitman, Slim, 192
Wichita Indian Reservation, 9
Wightman, John, 154
Wild Cat, Chief, 208
Wilkes, Robert, 222
Wilkinson, General James, 23,
30-31
Wilkinson, Jane, see Jane Long
Willacy County, 180, 248
Willacy, John G., 248
Williams, Samuel May, 150,
168-171
Williamson County, 171, 183
Wills, Bob, 192
Wilson County, 153

Winchester Arms Co., 190
Winnsboro, TX, 293
Wise County, 236
Women: Convicts, 218; state
    government, 219; Pro
    baseball, 196
Woodbury's colony, 150
World War I, 284, 287
World War II, 196, 238, 280,
    319-320
Wright Brothers, 285
Wright, Governor Silas, 261
Wright, George W., 117

Wrigley, Philip K., 196

X

XIT Ranch, 243

Y

YMCA (Young Men's Christian
    Association), 186
Young Territory, 243
Yucatan, 53, 92

Z

Zavala, Lorenzo de, 150
Zavalla, TX, 180, 182

About the Artist-Author

Patrick M. Reynolds researches, writes, and illustrates "Texa Lore" which appears every Sunday in the Texas and Southwes section of the *Dallas Morning News*. He also does another his torical cartoon called "Flashbacks" that runs in the Sunda color comics section of the *Washington Post* and other newspo pers. He did a similar illustrated history feature on New Yor called "Big Apple Almanac" that ran for eleven years in *Ne York Newsday*, and was published in three volumes, and "Penn sylvania Profiles" that appeared in over thirty publications fo fifteen years.

Reynolds has a Master of Fine Arts degree from Syracuse Un versity. He served as a military intelligence officer in th Vietnam War and was an instructor in the Command and General Staff Officers Course. He retired from the Army Reserve as a lieutenant colonel.